THE STORY
OF
A BAD BOY

THE *Story* OF A

BAD BOY

By

THOMAS BAILEY ALDRICH

Illustrated by
REGINALD MARSH

PANTHEON BOOKS

The text in this book is based on *Our Young Folks, an Illustrated Magazine for Boys and Girls, Boston, Fields, Osgood & Co.*, 1869.

CONTENTS

THE STORY
OF
A BAD BOY

ONE

IN WHICH I INTRODUCE MYSELF

THIS is the story of a bad boy. Well, not such a very bad, but a pretty bad boy; and I ought to know, for I am, or rather was, that boy myself.

Lest the title should mislead the reader, I hasten to assure him here that I have no dark confessions to make. I call my story the story of a bad boy, partly to distinguish myself from those faultless young gentlemen who generally figure in narratives of this kind, and partly because I really was *not* a cherub. I may truthfully say I was an amiable, impulsive lad, blessed with fine digestive powers, and no hypocrite. I didn't want to be an angel and with the angels stand; I didn't think the missionary tracts presented to me by the Rev. Wibird Hawkins were half so nice as Robinson Crusoe; and I didn't send my little pocket money to the natives of the Fiji Islands, but spent it royally in peppermint drops and taffy candy. In short, I was a real human boy, such as you may meet anywhere in New England, and no more like the impossible boy in a storybook than a sound orange is like one that has been sucked dry. But let us begin at the beginning.

Whenever a new scholar came to our school, I used to confront him at recess with the following words: "My name's Tom Bailey; what's your name?" If the name struck me favorably, I shook hands with the new pupil cordially; but if it didn't, I would turn on my heel, for I was particular on this point. Such names as Higgins, Wiggins, and Spriggins were deadly affronts to my ear; while Langdon, Wallace, Blake, and the like, were passwords to my confidence and esteem.

Ah me! some of those dear fellows are rather elderly boys by this time—lawyers, merchants, sea captains, soldiers, authors, what not? Phil Adams (a special good name that Adams) is consul at Shanghai, where I picture him to myself with his head closely shaved—he never had too much hair—and a long pigtail hanging down behind. He is married, I hear; and I hope he and she that was Miss Wang Wang are very happy together, sitting cross-legged over their diminutive cups of tea in a sky-blue tower hung with bells. It is so I think of him; to me he is henceforth a jeweled mandarin, talking nothing but broken China. Whitcomb is a judge, sedate and wise, with spectacles balanced on the bridge of that remarkable nose which, in former days, was so plentifully sprinkled with freckles that the boys christened him Pepper Whitcomb. Just to think of little Pepper Whitcomb being a judge! What would he do to me now, I wonder, if I were to sing out "Pepper!" some day in court? Fred Langdon is in California, in the native wine business,—he used to make the best licorice water *I* ever tasted! Binny Wallace sleeps in the Old South Burying Ground; and Jack Harris, too, is dead—Harris, who commanded us boys, of old, in the famous snowball battles of Slatter's Hill. Was it yesterday I saw him at the head of his regiment on its way to join the shattered Army of the Potomac? Not yesterday, but five years ago. It was at the battle of the Seven Pines. Gallant Jack Harris, that never drew rein until he had dashed into the Rebel battery! So they found him—lying across the enemy's guns.

How we have parted, and wandered, and married, and died! I wonder what has become of all the boys who went to the Temple Grammar School at Rivermouth when I was a youngster?

All, all are gone, the old familiar faces!

It is with no ungentle hand I summon them back, for a moment, from that Past which has closed upon them and upon me. How pleasantly they live again in my memory! Happy, magical Past, in whose fairy atmosphere even Conway, mine ancient foe, stands forth transfigured, with a sort of dreamy glory encircling his bright red hair!

With the old school formula I commence these sketches of my boyhood. My name is Tom Bailey; what is yours, gentle reader? I take for granted it is neither Wiggins nor Spriggins, and that we shall get on famously together in the pages of this magazine, and be capital friends forever.

TWO

IN WHICH I ENTERTAIN
PECULIAR VIEWS

I WAS born at Rivermouth, but before I had a chance to become very well acquainted with that pretty New England town, my parents removed to New Orleans, where my father invested his money so securely in the banking business that he was never able to get any of it out again. But of this hereafter. I was only eighteen months old at the time of the removal, and it didn't make much difference to me where I was, because I was so small; but several years later, when my father proposed to take me North to be educated, I had my own peculiar views on the subject. I instantly kicked over the little Negro boy who happened to be standing by me at the moment, and, stamping my foot violently on the floor of the piazza, declared that I would not be taken away to live among a lot of Yankees!

You see I was what is called "a Northern man with Southern principles." I had no recollection of New England; my earliest memories were connected with the South, with Aunt Chloe, my old Negro nurse, and with the great ill-kept garden in the center of which stood our house—a whitewashed stone house it was, with wide verandas—

6

shut out from the street by lines of orange and magnolia trees. I knew I was born in the North, but hoped nobody would find it out. I looked upon the misfortune as something so shrouded by time and distance that maybe nobody remembered it. I never told my schoolmates I was a Yankee, because they talked about the Yankees in such a scornful way it made me feel that it was quite a disgrace not to be born in Louisiana, or at least in one of the Border States. And this impression was strengthened by Aunt Chloe, who said, "dar wasn't no gentl'men in de Norf no way," and on one occasion terrified me beyond measure by declaring that, "if any of dem mean whites tried to git her away from marster, she was jes' gwine to knock 'em on de head wid a gourd!"

The way this poor creature's eyes flashed, and the tragic air with which she struck at an imaginary "mean white," are among the most vivid things in my memory of those days.

To be frank, my idea of the North was about as accurate as that entertained by the well-educated Englishman of the present day concerning America. I supposed the inhabitants were divided into two classes—Indians and white people; that the Indians occasionally dashed down on New York, and scalped any woman or child (giving the preference to children) whom they caught lingering in the outskirts after nightfall; that the white men were either hunters or schoolmasters, and that it was winter pretty much all the year round. The prevailing style of architecture I took to be log cabins.

With this delightful picture of Northern civilization in my eye, the reader will easily understand my terror at the bare thought of being transported to Rivermouth to school, and possibly will forgive me for kicking over little black Sam, and otherwise misconducting myself, when my father announced his determination to me. As for kicking little Sam—I *always* did that, more or less gently, when anything went wrong with me.

My father was greatly perplexed and troubled by this unusually violent outbreak, and especially by the real consternation which he saw written in every line of my countenance. As little black Sam picked himself up, my father took my hand in his and led me thoughtfully to the library.

I can see him now as he leaned back in the bamboo chair and questioned me. He appeared strangely agitated on learning the nature of my objections to going North, and proceeded at once to knock down all my pine-log houses, and scatter all the Indian tribes with which I had populated the greater portion of the Eastern and Middle States.

"Who on earth, Tom, has filled your brain with such silly stories?" asked my father, wiping the tears from his eyes.

"Aunt Chloe, sir; she told me."

"And you really thought your grandfather wore a blanket embroidered with beads, and ornamented his leggins with the scalps of his enemies?"

"Well, sir, I didn't think that exactly."

"Didn't think that exactly? Tom, you will be the death of me."

He hid his face in his handkerchief, and, when he looked up, he seemed to have been suffering acutely. I was deeply moved myself, though I did not clearly understand what I had said or done to cause him to feel so badly. Perhaps I

had hurt his feelings by thinking it even possible that
Grandfather Nutter was an Indian warrior.

My father devoted that evening and several subsequent
evenings to giving me a clear and succinct account of New
England; its early struggles, its progress, and its present
condition—faint and confused glimmerings of all which
I had obtained at school, where history had never been a
favorite pursuit of mine.

I was no longer unwilling to go North; on the contrary,
the proposed journey to a new world full of wonders kept
me awake nights. I promised myself all sorts of fun and
adventures, though I was not entirely at rest in my mind
touching the savages, and secretly resolved to go on

board the ship—the journey was to be made by sea—with
a certain little brass pistol in my trousers pocket, in case
of any difficulty with the tribes when we landed at Boston.

I couldn't get the Indian out of my head. Only a short
time previously the Cherokees—or was it the Comanches?
—had been removed from their hunting grounds in Ar-
kansas; and in the wilds of the southwest the red men
were still a source of terror to the border settlers. "Trouble with the Indians" was the staple news from Florida
published in the New Orleans papers. We were constantly
hearing of travelers being attacked and murdered in the
interior of that state. If these things were done in Florida,
why not in Massachusetts?

Yet long before the sailing day arrived I was eager to
be off. My impatience was increased by the fact that my
father had purchased for me a fine little Mustang pony,
and shipped it to Rivermouth a fortnight previous to the
date set for our own departure—for both my parents were
to accompany me. This pony (which nearly kicked me out
of bed one night in a dream), and my father's promise
that he and my mother would come to Rivermouth every
other summer, completely resigned me to the situation.
The pony's name was *Gitana*, which is the Spanish for
gypsy; so I always called her—she was a lady pony—
Gypsy.

At length the time came to leave the vine-covered mansion among the orange trees, to say good-by to little black
Sam (I am convinced he was heartily glad to get rid of
me), and to part with simple Aunt Chloe, who, in the confusion of her grief, kissed an eyelash into my eye, and then
buried her face in the bright bandanna turban which she
had mounted that morning in honor of our departure.

I fancy them standing by the open garden gate; the tears are rolling down Aunt Chloe's cheeks; Sam's six front teeth are glistening like pearls; I wave my hand to him manfully, then I call out "good-by" in a muffled voice to Aunt Chloe; they and the old home fade away. I am never to see them again!

THREE

ON BOARD THE TYPHOON

I DO not remember much about the voyage to Boston, for after the first few hours at sea I was dreadfully unwell.

The name of our ship was the "A No. 1, fast-sailing packet *Typhoon*." I learned afterwards that she sailed fast only in the newspaper advertisements. My father owned one quarter of the *Typhoon*, and that is why we happened to go in her. I tried to guess which quarter of the ship he owned, and finally concluded it must be the hind quarter—the cabin, in which we had the cosiest of staterooms, with one round window in the roof and two shelves or boxes nailed up against the wall to sleep in.

There was a good deal of confusion on deck while we were getting under way. The captain shouted orders (to which nobody seemed to pay any attention) through a battered tin trumpet, and grew so red in the face that he reminded me of a scooped-out pumpkin with a lighted candle inside. He swore right and left at the sailors without the slightest regard for their feelings. They didn't mind it a bit, however, but went on singing—

"Heave ho!
With the rum below.
And hurrah for the Spanish Main O!"

I will not be positive about "the Spanish Main," but it was hurrah for something O. I considered them very jolly fellows, and so indeed they were. One weatherbeaten tar in particular struck my fancy—a thick-set jovial man, about fifty years of age, with twinkling blue eyes and a fringe of gray hair circling his head like a crown. As he took off his tarpaulin I observed that the top of his head was quite smooth and flat, as if somebody had sat down on him when he was very young.

There was something noticeably hearty in this man's bronzed face, a heartiness that seemed to extend to his loosely knotted neckerchief. But what completely won my good will was a picture of enviable loveliness painted on his left arm. It was the head of a woman with the body of a fish. Her flowing hair was of livid green, and she held a pink comb in one hand. I never saw anything so beautiful. I determined to know that man. I think I would have given my brass pistol to have had such a picture painted on my arm.

While I stood admiring this work of art, a fat, wheezy steam tug, with the word AJAX in staring black letters on the paddle-box, came puffing up alongside the *Typhoon*. It was ridiculously small and conceited, compared with our stately ship. I speculated as to what it was going to do. In a few minutes we were lashed to the little monster, which gave a snort and a shriek, and commenced backing us out from the levee (wharf) with the greatest ease.

I once saw an ant running away with a piece of cheese eight or ten times larger than itself. I could not help thinking of it, when I found the chubby, smoky-nosed tugboat towing the *Typhoon* out into the Mississippi River.

In the middle of the stream we swung round, the current caught us, and away we flew like a great winged bird. Only it didn't seem as if *we* were moving. The shore, with the countless steamboats, the tangled rigging of the ships, and the long lines of warehouses, appeared to be gliding away from us.

It was grand sport to stand on the quarterdeck and watch all this. Before long there was nothing to be seen on either side but stretches of low swampy land, covered with stunted cypress trees, from which drooped delicate streamers of Spanish moss—a fine place for alligators and congo snakes. Here and there we passed a yellow sand bar, and here and there a snag lifted its nose out of the water like a shark.

"This is your last chance to see the city, Tom," said my father, as we swept round a bend of the river.

I turned and looked. New Orleans was just a colorless mass of something in the sunset, and the dome of the St. Charles Hotel, upon which the sun shimmered for a moment, was no bigger than the top of old Aunt Chloe's thimble.

What do I remember next? The gray sky and the fretful blue waters of the Gulf. The steam tug had long since let slip her hawsers, and gone panting away with a derisive scream, as much as to say, "I've done my duty, now look out for yourself, old *Typhoon!*"

The ship seemed quite proud of being left to take care of itself, and, with its huge white sails bulged out, strutted off like a vain turkey. I had been standing by my father near the wheelhouse all this while, observing things with that nicety of perception which belongs only to children; but now the dew began falling, and we went below to have supper.

The fresh fruit and milk, and the slices of cold chicken, looked very nice; yet somehow I had no appetite. There was a general smell of tar about everything. Then the ship gave sudden lurches that made it a matter of uncertainty whether one was going to put his fork to his mouth or into his eye. The tumblers and wineglasses, stuck in a rack over the table, kept clinking and clinking; and the cabin lamp, suspended by four gilt chains from the ceiling, swayed to and fro crazily. Now the floor seemed to rise, and now it seemed to sink under one's feet like a feather bed.

There were not more than a dozen passengers on board, including ourselves; and all of these, excepting a bald-headed old gentleman—a retired sea captain—disappeared into their staterooms at an early hour of the evening.

After supper was cleared away, my father and the elderly gentleman, whose name was Captain Truck,

played at checkers; and I amused myself for a while by watching the trouble they had in keeping the men in the proper places. Just at the most exciting point of the game, the ship would careen, and down would go the white checkers pell-mell among the black. Then my father laughed, but Captain Truck would grow very angry, and vow that he would have won the game in a move or two more, if the confounded old chicken coop—that's what he called the ship—hadn't lurched.

"I—I think I will go to bed now, please," I said, laying my hand on my father's knee, and feeling exceedingly queer.

It was high time, for the *Typhoon* was plunging about

in the most alarming fashion. I was speedily tucked away in the upper berth, where I felt a trifle more easy at first. My clothes were placed on a narrow shelf at my feet, and it was a great comfort to me to know that my pistol was so handy, for I made no doubt we should fall in with pirates before many hours. This is the last thing I remember with any distinctness. At midnight, as I was afterwards told, we were struck by a gale which never left us until we came in sight of the Massachusetts coast.

For days and days I had no sensible idea of what was going on around me. That we were being hurled somewhere upside down, and that I didn't like it, was about all I knew. I have, indeed, a vague impression that my father used to climb up to the berth and call me his "Ancient Mariner," bidding me cheer up. But the Ancient Mariner was far from cheering up, if I recollect rightly; and I don't believe that venerable navigator would have cared much if it had been announced to him, through a speaking-trumpet, that "a low, black, suspicious craft, with raking masts, was rapidly bearing down upon us!"

In fact, one morning, I thought that such was the case, for bang! went the big cannon I had noticed in the bow of the ship when we came on board, and which had suggested to me the idea about pirates. Bang! went the gun again in a few seconds. I made a feeble effort to get at my trousers pocket! But the *Typhoon* was only saluting Cape Cod—the first land sighted by vessels approaching the coast from a southerly direction.

The vessel had ceased to roll, and my seasickness passed away as rapidly as it came. I was all right now, "only a little shaky in my timbers and a little blue about the gills," as Captain Truck remarked to my mother, who, like myself, had been confined to the stateroom during the passage.

At Cape Cod the wind parted company with us without saying so much as "Excuse me"; so we were nearly two days in making the run which in favorable weather is usually accomplished in seven hours. That's what the pilot said.

I was able to go about the ship now, and I lost no time in cultivating the acquaintance of the sailor with the green-haired lady on his arm. I found him in the forecastle—a sort of cellar in the front part of the vessel. He was an agreeable sailor, as I had expected, and we became the best of friends in five minutes.

He had been all over the world two or three times, and knew no end of stories. According to his own account, he must have been shipwrecked at least twice a year ever since his birth. He had served under Decatur when that gallant officer peppered the Algerines and made them promise not to sell their prisoners of war into slavery; he had worked a gun at the bombardment of Vera Cruz in the Mexican War, and he had been on Alexander Selkirk's island more than once. There were very few things he hadn't done in a seafaring way.

"I suppose, sir," I remarked, "that *your* name isn't Typhoon?"

"Why, Lord love ye, lad, my name's Benjamin Watson, of Nantucket. But I'm a true-blue Typhooner," he added, which increased my respect for him; I don't know why, and I didn't know then whether Typhoon was the name of a vegetable or a profession.

Not wishing to be outdone in frankness, I disclosed to

him that *my* name was Tom Bailey, upon which he said
he was very glad to hear it.

When we got more intimate, I discovered that Sailor
Ben, as he wished me to call him, was a perfect walking
picture book. He had two anchors, a star, and a frigate

in full sail on his right arm; a pair of lovely blue hands
clasped on his breast, and I've no doubt that other parts
of his body were illustrated in the same agreeable manner.
I imagine he was fond of drawings, and took this means
of gratifying his artistic taste. It was certainly very ingenious and convenient. A portfolio might be misplaced,
or dropped overboard; but Sailor Ben had his pictures
wherever he went, just as that eminent person **in the**
poem—

With rings on her fingers and bells on her toes—

was accompanied by music on all occasions.

The two hands on his breast, he informed me, consti-
tuted a tribute to the memory of a dead messmate from
whom he had parted years ago—and surely a more touching tribute was never engraved on a tombstone. This
caused me to think of my parting with old Aunt Chloe,
and I told him I should take it as a great favor indeed if
he would paint a pink hand and a black hand on my chest.
He said the colors were pricked into the skin with needles,
and that the operation was somewhat painful. I assured
him, in an offhand manner, that I didn't mind pain, and
begged him to set to work at once.

The simple-hearted fellow, who was probably not a
little vain of his skill, took me into the forecastle, and was
on the point of complying with my request, when my
father happened to look down the gangway—a circumstance that rather interfered with the decorative art.

I didn't have another opportunity of conferring alone
with Sailor Ben, for the next morning, bright and early,
we came in sight of the cupola of the Boston State House.

FOUR

RIVERMOUTH

IT WAS a beautiful May morning when the *Typhoon*
hauled up at Long Wharf. Whether the Indians were
not early risers, or whether they were away just then on a
warpath, I couldn't determine; but they did not appear
in any great force—in fact, did not appear at all.

In the remarkable geography which I never hurt myself with studying at New Orleans, was a picture representing the landing of the Pilgrim Fathers at Plymouth.
The Pilgrim Fathers, in rather odd hats and coats, are
seen approaching the savages; the savages, in no coats
or hats to speak of, are evidently undecided whether to
shake hands with the Pilgrim Fathers or to make one
grand rush and scalp the entire party. Now this scene
had so stamped itself on my mind, that, in spite of all my
father had said, I was prepared for some such greeting
from the aborigines. Nevertheless, I was not sorry to have
my expectations unfulfilled. By the way, speaking of the
Pilgrim Fathers, I often used to wonder why there was no
mention made of the Pilgrim Mothers.

While our trunks were being hoisted from the hold of the ship, I mounted on the roof of the cabin, and took a critical view of Boston. As we came up the harbor, I had noticed that the houses were huddled together on an immense hill, at the top of which was a large building, the State House, towering proudly above the rest, like an amiable mother hen surrounded by her brood of many-colored chickens. A closer inspection did not impress me very favorably. The city was not nearly so imposing as New Orleans, which stretches out for miles and miles, in the shape of a crescent, along the banks of the majestic river.

I soon grew tired of looking at the masses of houses, rising above one another in irregular tiers, and was glad my father did not propose to remain long in Boston. As I leaned over the rail in this mood, a measly-looking little boy with no shoes said that if I would come down on the wharf he'd lick me for two cents—not an exorbitant price. But I didn't go down. I climbed into the rigging, and stared at him. This, as I was rejoiced to observe, so exasperated him that he stood on his head on a pile of boards, in order to pacify himself.

The first train for Rivermouth left at noon. After a late breakfast on board the *Typhoon*, our trunks were piled upon a baggage wagon, and ourselves stowed away in a coach, which must have turned at least one hundred corners before it set us down at the railway station.

In less time than it takes to tell it, we were shooting across the country at a fearful rate—now clattering over a bridge, now screaming through a tunnel; here we cut a flourishing village in two, like a knife, and here we dived into the shadow of a pine forest. Before a fellow could tell where he was, he was somewhere else. Sometimes we glided along the edge of the ocean, and could see the sails of ships twinkling like bits of silver against the horizon; sometimes we dashed across rocky pasturelands where stupid-eyed cattle were loafing. It was fun to scare the lazy-looking cows that lay round in groups under the newly budded trees near the railroad track.

Whenever we approached a village, the engineer sounded his bell, and slackened the speed of the train; but we did not pause at any of the little brown stations on the route (they looked just like overgrown black-walnut clocks), though at every one of them a man popped out as if he were worked by machinery, and waved a red flag, and appeared as though he would like to have us stop. But we were an express train, and made no stoppages, excepting once or twice to give the engine a drink.

It is strange how the memory clings to some things. It is over twenty years since I took that first ride to Rivermouth, and yet, oddly enough, I remember as if it were yesterday, that, as we passed slowly through the village of Hampton, we saw two boys fighting behind a red barn. There was also a shaggy yellow dog, who looked as if he had commenced to unravel, barking himself all up into a knot with excitement. We had only a hurried glimpse of the battle—long enough, however, to see that the combatants were equally matched and very much in earnest. I am ashamed to say how many times since I have speculated as to which boy got licked. Maybe both the small rascals are dead now (not in consequence of the set-to, let us hope), or maybe they are married, and have pugnacious urchins of their own; yet to this day I sometimes find myself wondering how that fight turned out.

We had been riding perhaps two hours and a half, when we shot by a tall factory with a chimney resembling a church steeple; then the locomotive gave a scream, the engineer rung his bell, and we plunged into the twilight of a long wooden building, open at both ends. Here we stopped, and the conductor, thrusting his head in at the car door, cried out, "Passengers for Rivermouth!"

At last we had reached our journey's end. On the platform my father shook hands with a straight, brisk old gentleman whose face was very serene and rosy. He had on a white hat and a long swallow-tailed coat, the collar of which came clear up above his ears. He didn't look unlike a Pilgrim Father. This, of course, was Grandfather Nutter, at whose house I was born. My mother kissed him a great many times; and I was glad to see him myself, though I naturally did not feel very intimate with a person whom I had not seen since I was eighteen months old.

While we were getting into the double-seated wagon
which Grandfather Nutter had provided, I took the opportunity of asking after the health of the pony. The
pony had arrived all right ten days before, and was in
the stable at home, quite anxious to see me.

As we drove through the quiet old town, I thought
Rivermouth the prettiest place in the world; and I think
so still. The streets are long and wide, shaded by gigantic
American elms, whose drooping branches, interlacing
here and there, span the avenues with arches graceful
enough to be the handiwork of fairies. Many of the houses
have small flower gardens in front, gay with china asters,
and are substantially built, with massive chimney stacks
and protruding eaves. A beautiful river goes rippling by
the town, and, after turning and twisting among a lot
of tiny islands, empties itself into the sea.

The harbor is so fine that the largest ships can sail
directly up to the wharves and drop anchor. Only they
don't. Years ago it was a famous seaport. Princely fortunes were made in the West India trade; and in 1812,
when we were at war with Great Britain, any number of
privateers were fitted out at Rivermouth to prey upon
the merchant vessels of the enemy. Certain people grew
suddenly and mysteriously rich. A great many of "the
first families" of today do not care to trace their pedigree
back to the time when their grandsires owned shares in the
Matilda Jane, twenty-four guns. Well, well!

Few ships come to Rivermouth now. Commerce drifted
into other ports. The phantom fleet sailed off one day, and
never came back again. The crazy old warehouses are
empty; and barnacles and eel grass cling to the piles of
the crumbling wharfs, where the sunshine lies lovingly,

bringing out the faint spicy odor that haunts the place—
the ghost of the old dead West India trade!

During our ride from the station, I was struck, of
course, only by the general neatness of the houses and the
beauty of the elm trees lining the streets. I describe Rivermouth now as I came to know it afterwards.

Rivermouth is a very ancient town. In my day there
existed a tradition among the boys that it was here Christopher Columbus made his first landing on this continent.
I remember having the exact spot pointed out to me by
Pepper Whitcomb! One thing is certain, Captain John
Smith, who afterwards, according to the legend, married
Pocahontas—whereby he got Powhatan for a father-in-
law—explored the river in 1614, and was much charmed
by the beauty of Rivermouth, which at that time was
covered with wild strawberry vines.

Rivermouth figures prominently in all the colonial his-
tories. It was loyal to the English king as long as loyalty
was a virtue, and then turned round and helped to thrash
His Majesty with a readiness truly touching. Whenever
there is any fighting to be done, the Rivermouth men are
on the alert. Such has been their character for two hun-

dred and fifty years. Who can tell how many of the brave
fellows lie under the walls of Quebec, in the trenches at
Bunker Hill, in the dark woods of Chancellorsville? Outside the town is a mossy graveyard in which there have
been no interments these four generations. Here you can
read on quaintly sculptured tombstones the names of
doughty naval captains and bold horsemen whose bodies
lie elsewhere.

> Their bones are dust,
> And their good swords rust:
> Their souls are with the saints, I trust.*

Every other house in the place has its tradition more
or less grim and entertaining. If ghosts could flourish
anywhere, there are certain streets in Rivermouth that
would be full of them. I don't know of a town with so many
old houses. Let us linger, for a moment, in front of the
one which the Oldest Inhabitant is always sure to point
out to the curious stranger.

It is a square wooden edifice, with gambrel roof and
deep-set window-frames. Over the windows and doors
there used to be heavy carvings—oak leaves and acorns,
and angels' heads with wings spreading from the ears,
oddly jumbled together; but these ornaments and other
outward signs of grandeur have long since disappeared.
A peculiar interest attaches itself to this house, not because of its age, for it has not been standing quite a century; nor on account of its architecture, which is not
striking—but because of the illustrious men who at various periods have occupied its spacious chambers.

In 1770 it was an aristocratic hotel. At the left side of
the entrance stood a high post, from which swung the sign

* Altered from Coleridge.

of the Earl of Halifax. The landlord was a stanch royalist —that is to say, he believed in the king; and when the overtaxed colonies determined to throw off the British yoke, the adherents to the Crown held private meetings in one of the back rooms of the tavern. This irritated the rebels, as they were called; and one night they made an attack on the Earl of Halifax, tore down the signboard, broke in the window-sashes, and gave the landlord hardly time to make himself invisible over a fence in the rear.

For several months the shattered tavern remained deserted. At last the exiled innkeeper, on promising to do better, was allowed to return; a new sign, bearing the name of William Pitt, the friend of America, swung proudly from the doorpost, and the patriots were appeased. Here it was that the mail coach from Boston twice a week, for many a year, set down its load of travelers and gossip. For some of the details in this sketch, I am indebted to a recently published chronicle of those times.

It is 1782. The French fleet is lying in the harbor of Rivermouth, and eight of the principal officers, in white uniforms trimmed with gold lace, have taken up their quarters at the sign of the William Pitt. Who is this young and handsome officer now entering the door of the tavern? It is no less a personage than the Marquis Lafayette, who has come all the way from Providence to visit the French gentlemen boarding there. What a gallant-looking cavalier he is, with his quick eyes and coal-black hair! Forty years later he visited the spot again; his locks were gray and his step was feeble, but his heart held its young love for Liberty.

Who is this finely dressed traveler alighting from his coach-and-four, attended by servants in livery? Do you know that sounding name, written in big valorous letters on the Declaration of Independence—written as if by the hand of a giant? Can you not see it now?—

John Hancock

This is he.

Three young men, with their valet, are standing on the doorstep of the William Pitt, bowing politely, and inquiring in the most courteous terms in the world if they can be accommodated. It is the time of the French Revolution, and these are three sons of the Duke of Orleans —Louis Philippe and his two brothers. Louis Philippe never forgot his visit to Rivermouth. Years afterwards, when he was seated on the throne of France, he asked an American lady, who chanced to be at his court, if the pleasant old mansion was still standing.

But a greater and a better man than the king of the French has honored this roof. Here, in 1789, came George Washington, the President of the United States, to pay his final complimentary visit to the state dignitaries. The wainscoted chamber where he slept, and the dining-hall where he entertained his guests, have a certain dignity and sanctity which even the present Irish tenants cannot wholly destroy.

During the period of *my* reign at Rivermouth, an ancient lady, Dame Jocelyn by name, lived in one of the upper rooms of this notable building. She was a dashing young belle at the time of Washington's first visit to the town, and must have been exceedingly coquettish and pretty, judging from a certain portrait on ivory still in the possession of the family. According to Dame Jocelyn, George Washington flirted with her just a little bit—in what a stately and highly finished manner can be imagined. There was a mirror with a deep filigreed frame hanging over the mantelpiece in this room. The glass was cracked and the quicksilver rubbed off or discolored in many places. When it reflected your face you had the singular pleasure of not recognizing yourself. It gave your features the appearance of having been run through a mincemeat machine. But what rendered the looking glass a thing of enchantment to me was a faded green feather, tipped with scarlet, which drooped from the top of the tarnished gilt moldings. This feather Washington took from the plume of his three-cornered hat, and presented with his own hand to the worshipful Mistress Jocelyn the day he left Rivermouth forever. I wish I could describe the mincing genteel air, and the ill-concealed self-complacency, with which the dear old lady related the incident.

Many a Saturday afternoon have I climbed up the rickety staircase to that dingy room, which always had a flavor of snuff about it, to sit on a stiff-backed chair and listen for hours together to Dame Jocelyn's stories of the olden time. How she would prattle! She was bed-

ridden—poor creature!—and had not been out of the
chamber for fourteen years. Meanwhile the world had
shot ahead of Dame Jocelyn. The changes that had taken
place under her very nose were unknown to this faded,
crooning old gentlewoman, whom the eighteenth century
had neglected to take away with the rest of its odd traps.
She had no patience with new-fangled notions. The old
ways and the old times were good enough for her. She had
never seen a steam engine, though she had heard "the
dratted thing" screech in the distance. In *her* day, when
gentlefolk traveled, they went in their own coaches. She
didn't see how respectable people could bring themselves
down to "riding in a car with rag-tag and bobtail and
Lord-knows-who." Poor old aristocrat! the landlord
charged her no rent for the room, and the neighbors took
turns in supplying her with meals. Towards the close of
her life—she lived to be ninety-nine—she grew very fretful and capricious about her food. If she didn't chance to
fancy what was sent her, she had no hesitation in sending
it back to the giver with "Miss Jocelyn's respectful com-
pliments."

But I have been gossiping too long—and yet not too
long if I have impressed upon the reader an idea of what
a rusty, delightful old town it was to which I had come
to spend the next three or four years of my boyhood.

A drive of twenty minutes from the station brought us
to the doorstep of Grandfather Nutter's house. What
kind of house it was, and what sort of people lived in it,
shall be told in another chapter.

FIVE

THE NUTTER HOUSE AND THE
NUTTER FAMILY

THE Nutter House—all the more prominent dwellings in Rivermouth are named after somebody; for instance, there is the Walford House, the Venner House, the Trefethern House, etc., though it by no means follows that they are inhabited by the people whose names they bear—the Nutter House, to resume, has been in our family nearly a hundred years, and is an honor to the builder (an ancestor of ours, I believe), supposing durability to be a merit. If our ancestor *was* a carpenter, he knew his

33

trade. I wish I knew mine as well. Such timber and such workmanship don't often come together in houses built nowadays.

Imagine a low-studded structure, with a wide hall running through the middle. At your right hand, as you enter, stands a tall black mahogany clock, looking like an Egyptian mummy set up on end. On each side of the hall are doors (whose knobs, it must be confessed, do not turn very easily), opening into large rooms wainscoted and rich in wood carvings about the mantelpieces and cornices. The walls are covered with pictured paper, representing landscapes and sea views. In the parlor, for example, this enlivening figure is repeated all over the room: a group of English peasants, wearing Italian hats, are dancing on a lawn that abruptly resolves itself into a sea beach, upon which stands a flabby fisherman (nationality unknown), quietly hauling in what appears to be a small whale, and totally regardless of the dreadful naval combat going on just beyond the end of his fishing-rod. On the other side of the ships is the mainland again, with the same peasants dancing. Our ancestors were very worthy people, but their wallpapers were abominable.

There are neither grates nor stoves in these quaint chambers, but splendid open chimney places, with room enough for the corpulent back log to turn over comfortably on the polished andirons. A wide staircase leads from the hall to the second story, which is arranged much like the first. Over this is the garret. I needn't tell a New England boy what a museum of curiosities is the garret of a well-regulated New England house of fifty or sixty years' standing. Here meet together, as if by some pre-

concerted arrangement, all the broken-down chairs of the
household, all the spavined tables, all the seedy hats, all
the intoxicated-looking boots, all the split walking sticks
that have retired from business, "weary with the march
of life." The pots, the pans, the trunks, the bottles—who

may hope to make an inventory of the numberless odds
and ends collected in this bewildering lumber room? But
what a place it is to sit of an afternoon with the rain pat-
tering on the roof! what a place in which to read *Gulliver's
Travels*, or the famous adventures of Rinaldo Rinaldini!

My grandfather's house stood a little back from the
main street, in the shadow of two handsome elms, whose
overgrown boughs would dash themselves against the
gables whenever the wind blew hard. In the rear was a
pleasant garden, covering perhaps a quarter of an acre,
full of purple plum trees and gooseberry bushes. These
trees were old settlers, and are all dead now, excepting
one, which bears a plum as big as an egg. This tree, as I
have said, is still standing, and a more beautiful tree to
tumble out of never grew anywhere. In the northwestern

corner of the garden were the stables and carriage house, opening upon a narrow lane. You may imagine that I made an early visit to that locality to inspect Gypsy. Indeed, I paid her a visit every half-hour during the first day of my arrival. At the twenty-fourth visit, she trod on my foot rather heavily, as a reminder, probably, that I was wearing out my welcome. She was a knowing little pony, that Gypsy, and I shall have much to say of her in the course of these pages.

Gypsy's quarters were very nice, but nothing among my new surroundings gave me more satisfaction than the cosy sleeping apartment that had been prepared for myself. It was the hall room over the front door.

I had never had a chamber all to myself before, and this one, about twice the size of our stateroom on board the *Typhoon*, was a marvel of neatness and comfort. Pretty chintz curtains hung at the window, and a patch quilt of more colors than were in Jacob's coat covered the little truckle-bed. The pattern of the wallpaper left nothing to be desired in that line. On a gray background were small bunches of leaves, unlike any that ever grew in this world; and on every other bunch perched a yellow bird, pitted with crimson spots, as if it had just recovered from a severe attack of the smallpox. That no such bird ever existed did not detract from my admiration of each one. There were two hundred and sixty-eight of these birds in all, not counting those split in two where the paper was badly joined. I counted them once when I was laid up with a fine black eye, and, falling asleep immediately dreamed that the whole flock suddenly took wing and flew out of the window. From that time I was never able to regard them as merely inanimate objects.

A washstand in the corner, a chest of carved mahogany
drawers, a looking-glass in a filigreed frame, and a high-
backed chair studded with brass nails like a coffin, con-
stituted the furniture. Over the head of the bed were two
oak shelves, holding perhaps a dozen books—among
which were *Theodore, or The Peruvians; Robinson Crusoe;* an odd volume of *Tristram Shandy;* Baxter's *Saints'
Rest;* and a fine English edition of the *Arabian Nights,*
with six hundred woodcuts by Harvey.

Shall I ever forget the hour when I first overhauled
these books? I do not allude especially to Baxter's *Saints'
Rest,* which is far from being a lively work for the young,
but to the *Arabian Nights,* and particularly to *Robinson
Crusoe.* The thrill that ran into my fingers' ends then has
not run out yet. Many a time did I steal up to this nest of
a room, and, taking the dog-eared volume from its shelf,
glide off into an enchanted realm, where there were no
lessons to get and no boys to smash my kite. In a lidless
trunk in the garret I subsequently unearthed another
motley collection of novels and romances, embracing the
adventures of Baron Trenck, Jack Sheppard, Don Quixote, Gil Blas, and Charlotte Temple—all of which I fed
upon like a bookworm.

I never come across a copy of any of those works without feeling a certain tenderness for the yellow-haired little
rascal who used to lean above the magic pages hour after
hour, religiously believing every word he read, and no
more doubting the reality of Sinbad the Sailor, or the
Knight of the Sorrowful Countenance, than he did the
existence of his own grandfather.

Against the wall at the foot of the bed hung a single-
barrel shotgun—placed there by Grandfather Nutter,

who knew what a boy loved, if ever a grandfather did. As the trigger of the gun had been
accidentally twisted off, it was not, perhaps, the
most dangerous weapon that could be placed in
the hands of youth. In this maimed condition
its "bump of destructiveness" was much less
than that of my small brass pocket pistol, which
I at once proceeded to suspend from one of the
nails supporting the fowling-piece, for my va-
garies concerning the red man had been entirely
dispelled.

Having introduced the reader to the Nutter
House, a presentation to the Nutter family
naturally follows. The family consisted of my
grandfather; his sister, Miss Abigail Nutter;
and Kitty Collins, the maid-of-all-work.

Grandfather Nutter was a hale, cheery old
gentleman, as straight and as bald as an arrow.
He had been a sailor in early life; that is to say,
at the age of ten he fled from the multiplication
table, and ran away to sea. A single voyage
satisfied him. There never was but one of our
family who didn't run away to sea, and this
one died at his birth. My grandfather had also
been a soldier—a captain of militia in 1812. If
I owe the British nation anything, I owe thanks
to that particular British soldier who put a
musket ball into the fleshy part of Captain
Nutter's leg, causing that noble warrior a slight
permanent limp, but offsetting the injury by
furnishing him with the material for a story
which the old gentleman was never weary of

telling and I never weary of listening to. The story, in
brief, was as follows: At the breaking out of the war, an
English frigate lay for several days off the coast near
Rivermouth. A strong fort defended the harbor, and a

regiment of minute-men, scattered at various points along
shore, stood ready to repel the boats, should the enemy try
to effect a landing. Captain Nutter had charge of a slight
earthwork just outside the mouth of the river. Late one
thick night the sound of oars was heard; the sentinel tried
to fire off his gun at half-cock, and couldn't, when Captain Nutter sprang upon the parapet in the pitch darkness, and shouted, "Boat ahoy!" A musket shot immediately embedded itself in the calf of his leg. The Captain
tumbled into the fort, and the boat, which had probably
come in search of water, pulled back to the frigate.

This was my grandfather's only exploit during the war.
That his prompt and bold conduct was instrumental in

teaching the enemy the hopelessness of attempting to conquer such a people was among the firm beliefs of my boyhood.

At the time I came to Rivermouth, my grandfather had retired from active pursuits, and was living at ease on his money, invested principally in shipping. He had been a widower many years; a maiden sister, the aforesaid Miss Abigail, managing his household. Miss Abigail also managed her brother, and her brother's servant, and the visitor at her brother's gate—not in a tyrannical spirit, but from a philanthropic desire to be useful to everybody. In person she was tall and angular; she had a gray complexion, gray eyes, gray eyebrows, and generally wore a gray dress. Her strongest weak point was a belief in the efficacy of "hot drops" as a cure for all known diseases.

If there were ever two people who seemed to dislike each other, Miss Abigail and Kitty Collins were those people. If ever two people really loved each other, Miss Abigail and Kitty Collins were those people also. They were always either skirmishing or having a cup of tea lovingly together.

Miss Abigail was very fond of me, and so was Kitty; and in the course of their disagreements each let me into the private history of the other. According to Kitty, it was not originally my grandfather's intention to have Miss Abigail at the head of his domestic establishment. She had swooped down on him (Kitty's own words), with a bandbox in one hand and a faded blue cotton umbrella, still in existence, in the other. Clad in this singular garb— I do not remember that Kitty alluded to any additional peculiarity of dress—Miss Abigail had made her appearance at the door of the Nutter House on the morning of

my grandmother's funeral. The small amount of baggage
which the lady brought with her would have led the super-
ficial observer to infer that Miss Abigail's visit was limited
to a few days. I run ahead of my story in saying she remained seventeen years! How much longer she would have
remained can never be definitely known now, as she died
at the expiration of that period.

Whether or not my grandfather was quite pleased by
this unlooked-for addition to his family is a problem. He
was very kind always to Miss Abigail, and seldom opposed
her; though I think she must have tried his patience sometimes, especially when she interfered with Kitty.

Kitty Collins, or Mrs. Catherine, as she preferred to
be called, was descended in a direct line from an extensive
family of kings who formerly ruled over Ireland. In consequence of various calamities, among which the failure
of the potato crop may be mentioned, Miss Kitty Collins,
in company with several hundred of her countrymen and
countrywomen—also descended from kings—came over
to America in an emigrant ship, in the year eighteen hundred and something. I don't know what freak of fortune
caused the royal exile to turn up at Rivermouth; but turn
up she did, a few months after arriving in this country,
and was hired by my grandmother to do "general house-
work" for the sum of four shillings and sixpence a week.

Kitty had been living about seven years in my grandfather's family when she unburdened her heart of a secret
which had been weighing upon it all that time. It may be
said of people, as it is said of nations, "Happy are they
that have no history." Kitty had a history, and a pathetic
one, I think.

On board the emigrant ship that brought her to America, she became acquainted with a sailor, who, being touched by Kitty's forlorn condition, was very good to her. Long before the end of the voyage, which had been tedious and perilous, she was heartbroken at the thought of separating from her kindly protector; but they were

not to part just yet, for the sailor returned Kitty's affection, and the two were married on their arrival at port.

Kitty's husband—she would never mention his name, but kept it locked in her bosom like some precious relic—had a considerable sum of money when the crew were paid off; and the young couple—for Kitty was young then—lived very happily in a lodging house on South Street, near the docks. This was in New York.

The days flew by like hours, and the stocking in which the little bride kept the funds shrunk and shrunk, until at last there were only three or four dollars left in the toe of it. Then Kitty was troubled; for she knew her sailor would have to go to sea again unless he could get employment on shore. This he endeavored to do, but not with much success. One morning as usual he kissed her good day, and set out in search of work.

"Kissed me good-by, and called me his little Irish lass," sobbed Kitty, telling the story—"kissed me good-by, and, Heaven help me! I never set eye on him nor on the likes of him again!"

He never came back. Day after day dragged on, night after night, and then the weary weeks. What had become of him? Had he been murdered? had he fallen into the docks? had he—*deserted her?* No! she could not believe that; he was too brave and tender and true. She couldn't believe that. He was dead, dead, or he'd come back to her.

Meanwhile the landlord of the lodging house turned Kitty into the streets, now that "her man" was gone, and the payment of the rent doubtful. She got a place as a servant. The family she lived with shortly moved to Boston, and she accompanied them; then they went abroad, but Kitty would not leave America. Somehow she drifted to Rivermouth, and for seven long years never gave speech to her sorrow, until the kindness of strangers, who had become friends to her, unsealed the heroic lips.

Kitty's story, you may be sure, made my grandparents treat her more kindly than ever. In time she grew to be regarded less as a servant than as a friend in the home circle, sharing its joys and sorrows—a faithful nurse, a willing slave, a happy spirit in spite of all. I fancy I hear her singing over her work in the kitchen, pausing from time to time to make some witty reply to Miss Abigail— for Kitty, like all her race, had a vein of unconscious humor. Her bright honest face comes to me out from the past, the light and life of the Nutter House when I was a boy at Rivermouth.

LIGHTS AND SHADOWS

THE first shadow that fell upon me in my new home was caused by the return of my parents to New Orleans. Their visit was cut short by business which required my father's presence in Natchez, where he was establishing a branch of the banking house. When they had gone, a sense of loneliness such as I had never dreamed of filled my young breast. I crept away to the stable, and, throwing my arms about Gypsy's neck, sobbed aloud. She too had come from the sunny South, and was now a stranger in a strange land. The little mare seemed to realize our situation, and gave me all the sympathy I could ask, repeatedly rubbing her soft nose over my face and lapping up my salt tears with evident relish.

When night came, I felt still more lonesome. My grandfather sat in his armchair the greater part of the evening, reading the *Rivermouth Barnacle*, the local newspaper. There was no gas in those days, and the Captain read by the aid of a small block-tin lamp, which he held in one hand. I observed that he had a habit of dropping off into a doze every three or four minutes, and I forgot my homesickness at intervals in watching him. Two or three times,

45

to my vast amusement, he scorched the edges of the newspaper with the wick of the lamp; and at about half past
eight o'clock I had the satisfaction—I am sorry to confess
it was a satisfaction—of seeing the *Rivermouth Barnacle*
in flames.

My grandfather leisurely extinguished the fire with his
hands, and Miss Abigail, who sat near a low table, knit-
ting by the light of an astral lamp, did not even look up.
She was quite used to this catastrophe.

There was little or no conversation during the evening.
In fact, I do not remember that anyone spoke at all, excepting once, when the Captain remarked, in a meditative
manner, that my parents "must have reached New York
by this time"; at which supposition I nearly strangled
myself in attempting to intercept a sob.

The monotonous "click-click" of Miss Abigail's needles
made me nervous after a while, and finally drove me out
of the sitting-room into the kitchen, where Kitty caused
me to laugh by saying Miss Abigail thought that what I
needed was "a good dose of hot drops"—a remedy she was

forever ready to administer in all emergencies. If a boy broke his leg, or lost his mother, I believe Miss Abigail would have given him hot drops.

Kitty laid herself out to be entertaining. She told me several funny Irish stories, and described some of the odd people living in the town; but, in the midst of her comicalities, the tears would involuntarily ooze out of my eyes, though I was not a lad much addicted to weeping. Then Kitty would put her arms around me, and tell me not to mind it—that it wasn't as if I had been left alone in a foreign land with no one to care for me, like a poor girl whom she had once known. I brightened up before long, and told Kitty all about the *Typhoon* and the old seaman, whose name I tried in vain to recall, and was obliged to fall back on plain Sailor Ben.

I was glad when ten o'clock came, the bedtime for young folks, and old folks too, at the Nutter House. Alone in the hall chamber I had my cry out, once for all, moistening the pillow to such an extent that I was obliged to turn it over to find a dry spot to go to sleep on.

My grandfather wisely concluded to put me to school at once. If I had been permitted to go mooning about the house and stables I should have kept my discontent alive for months. The next morning, accordingly, he took me by the hand, and we set forth for the academy, which was located at the further end of the town.

The Temple School was a two-story brick building, standing in the center of a great square piece of land, surrounded by a high picket fence. There were three or four sickly trees, but no grass, in this enclosure, which had been worn smooth and hard by the tread of multitudinous feet. I noticed here and there small holes scooped in the ground, indicating that it was the season for marbles. A better playground for baseball couldn't have been devised.

On reaching the schoolhouse door, the Captain inquired for Mr. Grimshaw. The boy who answered our knock

ushered us into a side room, and in a few minutes—during which my eye took in forty-two caps hung on forty-two wooden pegs—Mr. Grimshaw made his appearance. He was a slender man, with white, fragile hands, and eyes that glanced half a dozen different ways at once—a habit probably acquired from watching the boys.

After a brief consultation, my grandfather patted me on the head and left me in charge of this gentleman, who seated himself in front of me and proceeded to sound the depth, or, more properly speaking, the shallowness, of my attainments. I suspect my historical information rather startled him. I recollect I gave him to understand that Richard III was the last king of England.

This ordeal over, Mr. Grimshaw rose and bade me follow him. A door opened, and I stood in the blaze of forty-two pairs of upturned eyes. I was a cool hand for my age, but I lacked the boldness to face this battery without wincing. In a sort of dazed way I stumbled after Mr.

Grimshaw down a narrow aisle between two rows of desks, and shyly took the seat pointed out to me.

The faint buzz that had floated over the schoolroom at our entrance died away, and the interrupted lessons were resumed. By degrees I recovered my coolness, and ventured to look around me. The owners of the forty-two caps were seated at small green desks like the one assigned to me. The desks were arranged in six rows, with spaces between just wide enough to prevent the boys' whispering. A blackboard set into the wall extended clear across the end of the room; on a raised platform near the door stood the master's table; and directly in front of this was a recitation bench capable of seating fifteen or twenty pupils. A pair of globes, tattooed with dragons and winged horses, occupied a shelf between two windows, which were so high from the floor that nothing but a giraffe could have looked out of them.

Having possessed myself of these details, I scrutinized my new acquaintances with unconcealed curiosity, instinctively selecting my friends and picking out my enemies—and in only two cases did I mistake my man.

A sallow boy with bright red hair, sitting in the fourth row, shook his fist at me furtively several times during the morning. I had a presentiment I should have trouble with that boy some day—a presentiment subsequently realized.

On my left was a chubby little fellow with a great many freckles (this was Pepper Whitcomb), who made some mysterious motions to me. I didn't understand them, but, as they were clearly of a pacific nature, I winked my eye at him. This appeared to be satisfactory, for he then went on with his studies. At recess he gave me the core of his apple, though there were several applicants for it.

Presently a boy in a loose olive-green jacket with two rows of brass buttons held up a folded paper behind his slate, intimating that it was intended for me. The paper was passed skillfully from desk to desk until it reached my hands. On opening the scrap, I found that it contained a small piece of molasses candy in an extremely humid state. This was certainly kind. I nodded my acknowledgments and hastily slipped the delicacy into my mouth. In a second I felt my tongue grow red hot with cayenne pepper. My face must have assumed a comical expression, for the boy in the olive-green jacket gave an hysterical laugh, for which he was instantly punished by Mr. Grimshaw. I swallowed the fiery candy, though it brought the water to my eyes, and managed to look so unconcerned that I was the only pupil in the form who escaped questioning as to the cause of Marden's misdemeanor. C. Marden was his name.

At recess several of the scholars came to my desk and shook hands with me, Mr. Grimshaw having previously introduced me to Phil Adams, charging him to see that I got into no trouble. My new acquaintances suggested that we should adjourn to the playground. We were no sooner out of doors than the boy with the red hair thrust his way through the crowd and placed himself at my side.

"I say, youngster, if you're comin' to this school you've got to toe the mark."

I didn't see any mark to toe, and didn't understand what he meant; but I replied politely that, if it was the custom of the school, I should be happy to toe the mark if he would point it out to me.

"I don't want any of your sarse," said the boy, scowling.

"Look here, Conway!" cried a clear voice from the other side of the playground, "you let young Bailey alone. He's a stranger here, and might be afraid of you, and thrash you. Why do you always throw yourself in the way of getting thrashed?"

I turned to the speaker, who by this time had reached the spot where we stood. Conway slunk off, favoring me with a parting scowl of defiance. I gave my hand to the boy who had befriended me—his name was Jack Harris—and thanked him for his good will.

"I tell you what it is, Bailey," he said, returning my pressure goodnaturedly, "you'll have to fight Conway before the quarter ends, or you'll have no rest. That fellow is always hankering after a licking, and of course you'll give him one by and by; but what's the use of hurrying up an unpleasant job? Let's have some baseball. By the way, Bailey, you were a good kid not to let on to Grimshaw about that candy. Charley Marden would have caught it twice as heavy. He's sorry he played the joke on you, and told me to tell you so. Hallo, Blake! where are the bats?"

This was addressed to a handsome, frank-looking lad of about my own age, who was engaged just then in cutting his initials on the bark of a tree near the schoolhouse. Blake shut up his penknife and went off to get the bats.

During the game which ensued I made the acquaintance of Charley Marden, Binny Wallace, Pepper Whitcomb, Harry Blake, and Fred Langdon. These boys, none of them more than a year or two older than I (Binny Wallace was younger), were ever after my chosen comrades. Phil Adams and Jack Harris were considerably our seniors, and, though they always treated us "kids" very kindly, they generally went with another set. Of course, before long I knew all the Temple boys more or less intimately, but the five I have named were my constant companions.

My first day at the Temple Grammar School was on the whole satisfactory. I had made several warm friends and only two permanent enemies—Conway and his echo, Seth Rodgers; for these two always went together, like a deranged stomach and a headache.

Before the end of the week I had my studies well in hand. I was a little ashamed at finding myself at the foot of the various classes, and secretly determined to deserve promotion. The school was an admirable one. I might make this part of my story more entertaining by picturing Mr. Grimshaw as a tyrant with a red nose and a large stick; but, unfortunately for the purposes of sensational narrative, Mr. Grimshaw was a quiet, kindhearted gentleman. Though a rigid disciplinarian, he had a keen sense of justice, was a good reader of character, and the boys respected him. There were two other teachers—a French tutor, and a writing master, who visited the school twice a week. On Wednesdays and Saturdays we were dismissed at noon, and these half-holidays were the brightest epochs of my existence.

Daily contact with boys who had not been brought up as gently as I worked an immediate, and, in some respects, a beneficial change in my character. I had the nonsense taken out of me, as the saying is—some of the nonsense, at least. I became more manly and self-reliant. I discovered that the world was not created exclusively on my account. In New Orleans I labored under the delusion that it was. Having neither brother nor sister to give up to at home, and being, moreover, the largest pupil at school there, my will had seldom been opposed. At Rivermouth matters were different, and I was not long in adapting myself to the altered circumstances. Of course I got many severe rubs, often unconsciously given; but I had the sense to see that I was all the better for them.

My social relations with my new schoolfellows were the pleasantest possible. There was always some exciting excursion on foot—a ramble through the pine woods, a visit to the Devil's Pulpit, a high cliff in the neighborhood—or a surreptitious row on the river, involving an exploration of a group of diminutive islands, upon one of which we pitched a tent and played we were the Spanish sailors who got wrecked there years ago. But the endless pine forest that skirted the town was our favorite haunt. There was a great green pond hidden somewhere in its depths, inhabited by a monstrous colony of turtles. Harry Blake, who had an eccentric passion for carving his name on everything, never let a captured turtle slip through his fingers without leaving his mark engraved on its shell. He must have lettered about two thousand from first to last. We used to call them Harry Blake's sheep. These turtles were of a discontented and migratory turn of mind, and we frequently encountered two or three of them on the crossroads several miles from their ancestral mud. Unspeakable was our delight whenever we discovered one soberly walking off with Harry Blake's initials! I've no doubt there are, at this moment, fat ancient turtles wandering about that gummy woodland with H. B. neatly cut on their venerable backs.

It soon became a custom among my playmates to make our barn their rendezvous. Gypsy proved a strong attraction. Captain Nutter bought me a little two-wheeled cart, which she drew quite nicely, after kicking out the dasher and breaking the shafts once or twice. With our lunch baskets and fishing tackle stowed away under the seat, we used to start off early in the afternoon for the seashore, where there were countless marvels in the shape of shells, mosses, and kelp. Gypsy enjoyed the sport as keenly as any of us, even going so far, one day, as to trot down the beach into the sea where we were bathing. As she took the cart with her, our provisions were not much improved. I shall never forget how squash pie tastes after being soused in the Atlantic Ocean. Soda crackers dipped in salt water are palatable, but not squash pie.

There was a good deal of wet weather during those first six weeks at Rivermouth, and we set ourselves at work to find some indoor amusement for our half-holidays. It was all very well for Amadis de Gaul and Don Quixote not to mind the rain; they had iron overcoats, and were not, from all we can learn, subject to croup and the guidance of their grandfathers. Our case was different.

"Now, boys, what shall we do?" I asked, addressing a thoughtful conclave of seven, assembled in our barn one dismal rainy afternoon.

"Let's have a theater," suggested Binny Wallace.

The very thing! But where? The loft of the stable was ready to burst with hay provided for Gypsy, but the long room over the carriage house was unoccupied. The place of all places! My managerial eye saw at a glance its capabilities for a theater. I had been to the play a great many times in New Orleans, and was wise in matters pertaining to the drama. So here, in due time, was set up some extraordinary scenery of my own painting. The curtain, I recollect, though it worked smoothly enough on other occasions, invariably hitched during the performances; and it often required the united energies of the Prince of Denmark, the King, and the Grave-digger, with an occasional hand from "the fair Ophelia" (Pepper Whitcomb in a low-necked dress), to hoist that bit of green cambric.

The theater, however, was a success, as far as it went. I retired from the business with no fewer than fifteen hundred pins, after deducting the headless, the pointless, and the crooked pins with which our doorkeeper frequently got "stuck." From first to last we took in a great deal of this counterfeit money. The price of admission to the "Rivermouth Theater" was twenty pins. I played all the principal parts myself—not that I was a finer actor than the other boys, but because I owned the establishment.

At the tenth representation, my dramatic career was brought to a close by an unfortunate circumstance. We were playing the drama of "William Tell, the Hero of Switzerland." Of course I was William Tell, in spite of Fred Langdon, who wanted to act that character himself. I wouldn't let him, so he withdrew from the company, taking the only bow and arrow we had. I made a crossbow out of a piece of whalebone, and did very well without him. We had reached that exciting scene where Gessler, the Austrian tyrant, commands Tell to shoot the apple from his son's head. Pepper Whitcomb, who played all the juvenile and women parts, was my son. To guard against mischance, a piece of pasteboard was fastened by a hand-kerchief over the upper portion of Whitcomb's face, while the arrow to be used was sewed up in a strip of flan-nel. I was a capital marksman, and the big apple, only two yards distant, turned its russet cheek fairly towards me.

I can see poor little Pepper now, as he stood without flinching, waiting for me to perform my great feat. I raised the crossbow amid the breathless silence of the crowded audience—consisting of seven boys and three girls, exclusive of Kitty Collins, who insisted on paying her way in with a clothespin. I raised the crossbow, I re-peat. Twang! went the whipcord; but, alas! instead of hitting the apple, the arrow flew right into Pepper Whit-comb's mouth, which happened to be open at the time, and destroyed my aim.

I shall never be able to banish that awful moment from my memory. Pepper's roar, expressive of astonishment, indignation, and pain, is still ringing in my ears. I looked upon him as a corpse, and, glancing not far into the dreary future, pictured myself led forth to execution in the presence of the very same spectators then assembled.

Luckily poor Pepper was not seriously hurt; but Grandfather Nutter, appearing in the midst of the con-fusion (attracted by the howls of young Tell), issued an injunction against all theatricals thereafter, and the place was closed; not, however, without a farewell speech from me, in which I said that this would have been the proudest moment of my life if I hadn't hit Pepper Whitcomb in the mouth. Whereupon the audience (assisted, I am glad to state, by Pepper) cried "Hear! hear!" I then attributed

the accident to Pepper himself, whose mouth, being open
at the instant I fired, acted upon the arrow much after the
fashion of a whirlpool, and drew in the fatal shaft. I was
about to explain how a comparatively small maelstrom
could suck in the largest ship, when the curtain fell of its
own accord, amid the shouts of the audience.

This was my last appearance on any stage. It was some
time, though, before I heard the end of the William Tell
business. Malicious little boys who hadn't been allowed to
buy tickets to my theater used to cry out after me in the
street—

> "Who killed Cock Robin?"
> "I," said the sparrer,
> "With my bow and arrer,
> I killed Cock Robin!"

The sarcasm of this verse was more than I could stand.
And it made Pepper Whitcomb pretty mad to be called
Cock Robin, I can tell you!

So the days glided on, with fewer clouds and more sunshine than fall to the lot of most boys. Conway was cer-

tainly a cloud. Within school bounds he seldom ventured
to be aggressive; but whenever we met about town he
never failed to brush against me, or pull my cap over my
eyes, or drive me distracted by inquiring after my family
in New Orleans, always alluding to them as highly respectable colored people.

Jack Harris was right when he said Conway would give
me no rest until I fought him. I felt it was ordained ages
before our birth that we should meet on this planet and
fight. With the view of not running counter to destiny, I
quietly prepared myself for the impending conflict. The
scene of my dramatic triumphs was turned into a gym-
nasium for this purpose, though I did not openly avow the
fact to the boys. By persistently standing on my head,
raising heavy weights, and going hand over hand up a
ladder, I developed my muscle until my little body was as
tough as a hickory knot and as supple as tripe. I also took
occasional lessons in the noble art of self-defense, under
the tuition of Phil Adams.

I brooded over the matter until the idea of fighting
Conway became a part of me. I fought him in imagination
during school hours; I dreamed of fighting with him at
night, when he would suddenly expand into a giant twelve
feet high, and then as suddenly shrink into a pygmy so
small that I couldn't hit him. In this latter shape he would
get into my hair, or pop into my waistcoat pocket, treat-
ing me with as little ceremony as the Lilliputians showed
Captain Lemuel Gulliver—all of which was not pleasant,
to be sure. On the whole, Conway was a cloud.

And then I had a cloud at home. It was not Grandfather
Nutter, nor Miss Abigail, nor Kitty Collins, though they
all helped to compose it. It was a vague, funereal, impal-

pable something which no amount of gymnastic training
would enable me to knock over. It was Sunday. If ever I
have a boy to bring up in the way he should go, I intend
to make Sunday a cheerful day to him. Sunday was *not*
a cheerful day at the Nutter House. You shall judge for
yourself.

It is Sunday morning. I should premise by saying that
the deep gloom which has settled over everything set in
like a heavy fog early on Saturday evening.

At seven o'clock my grandfather comes smilelessly down
stairs. He is dressed in black, and looks as if he had lost all
his friends during the night. Miss Abigail, also in black,
looks as if she were prepared to bury them, and not in-
disposed to enjoy the ceremony. Even Kitty Collins has
caught the contagious gloom, as I perceive when she
brings in the coffee urn—a solemn and sculpturesque urn
at any time, but monumental now—and sets it down in
front of Miss Abigail. Miss Abigail gazes at the urn as if
it held the ashes of her ancestors, instead of a generous
quantity of fine old Java coffee. The meal progresses in
silence.

Our parlor is by no means thrown open every day. It is open this June morning, and is pervaded by a strong smell of center table. The furniture of the room, and the little China ornaments on the mantelpiece, have a constrained, unfamiliar look. My grandfather sits in a mahogany chair, reading a large Bible covered with green baize. Miss Abigail occupies one end of the sofa, and has her hands crossed stiffly in her lap. I sit in the corner, crushed. Robinson Crusoe and Gil Blas are in close confinement. Baron Trenck, who managed to escape from the fortress of Glatz, can't for the life of him get out of our sitting-room closet. Even the *Rivermouth Barnacle* is suppressed until Monday. Genial converse, harmless books, smiles, lightsome hearts, all are banished. If I want to read anything, I can read Baxter's *Saints' Rest.* I would die first. So I sit there kicking my heels, thinking about New Orleans, and watching a morbid blue-bottle fly that attempts to commit suicide by butting his head against the windowpane. Listen!—no, yes—it is—it is the robins singing in the garden—the grateful, joyous robins singing away like mad, just as if it wasn't Sunday. Their audacity tickles me.

My grandfather looks up, and inquires in a sepulchral voice if I am ready for Sabbath school. It is time to go. I like the Sabbath school; there are bright young faces *there*, at all events. When I get out into the sunshine alone, I draw a long breath; I would turn a somersault up against Neighbor Penhallow's newly painted fence if I hadn't my best trousers on, so glad am I to escape from the oppressive atmosphere of the Nutter House.

Sabbath school over, I go to meeting, joining my grandfather, who doesn't appear to be any relation to me this day, and Miss Abigail, in the porch. Our minister holds out very little hope to any of us of being saved. Convinced that I am a lost creature, in common with the

human family, I return home behind my guardians at a snail's pace. We have a dead cold dinner. I saw it laid out yesterday.

There is a long interval between this repast and the second service, and a still longer interval between the beginning and the end of that service; for the Rev. Wibird Hawkins's sermons are none of the shortest, whatever else they may be.

After meeting, my grandfather and I take a walk. We visit—appropriately enough—a neighboring graveyard. I am by this time in a condition of mind to become a willing inmate of the place. The usual evening prayer meeting is postponed for some reason. At half past eight I go to bed.

This is the way Sunday was observed in the Nutter House, and pretty generally throughout the town, twenty years ago. People who were prosperous and natural and happy on Saturday became the most rueful of human beings in the brief space of twelve hours. I don't think there was any hypocrisy in this. It was merely the old Puritan austerity cropping out once a week. Many of these people were pure Christians every day in the seven—excepting the seventh. Then they were decorous and solemn to the verge of moroseness. I should not like to be misunderstood on this point. Sunday is a blessed day, and therefore it should not be made a gloomy one. It is the Lord's day, and I do believe that cheerful hearts and faces are not unpleasant in His sight.

O day of rest! How beautiful, how fair,
How welcome to the weary and the old!
Day of the Lord! and truce to earthly cares!
Day of the Lord, as all our days should be!
Ah, why will man by his austerities
Shut out the blessed sunshine and the light,
And make of thee a dungeon of despair!

ONE MEMORABLE NIGHT

TWO months had elapsed since my arrival at River-mouth, when the approach of an important celebration produced the greatest excitement among the juvenile population of the town.

There was very little hard study done in the Temple Grammar School the week preceding the Fourth of July. For my part, my heart and brain were so full of firecrackers, Roman candles, rockets, pinwheels, squibs, and gunpowder in various seductive forms, that I wonder I didn't explode under Mr. Grimshaw's very nose. I couldn't do a sum to save me; I couldn't tell, for love or money, whether Tallahassee was the capital of Tennessee or of Florida; the present and the pluperfect tenses were inextricably mixed in my memory, and I didn't know a verb from an adjective when I met one. This was not alone my condition, but that of every boy in the school.

Mr. Grimshaw considerably made allowances for our temporary distraction, and sought to fix our interest on the lessons by connecting them directly or indirectly with the coming Event. The class in arithmetic, for instance, was requested to state how many boxes of firecrackers,

63

each box measuring sixteen inches square, could be stored in a room of such and such dimensions. He gave us the Declaration of Independence for a parsing exercise, and in geography confined his questions almost exclusively to localities rendered famous in the Revolutionary war.

"What did the people of Boston do with the tea on board the English vessels?" asked our wily instructor.

"Threw it into the river!" shrieked the boys, with an impetuosity that made Mr. Grimshaw smile in spite of himself. One luckless urchin said, "Chucked it," for which happy expression he was kept in at recess.

Notwithstanding these clever stratagems, there was not much solid work done by anybody. The trail of the serpent (an inexpensive but dangerous fire toy) was over us all. We went round deformed by quantities of Chinese crackers artlessly concealed in our trousers pockets; and if a boy whipped out his handkerchief without proper precaution, he was sure to let off two or three torpedoes.

Even Mr. Grimshaw was made a sort of accessory to the universal demoralization. In calling the school to order, he always rapped on the table with a heavy ruler. Under the green baize tablecloth, on the exact spot where he usually struck, a certain boy, whose name I withhold, placed a fat torpedo. The result was a loud explosion, which caused Mr. Grimshaw to look queer. Charley Marden was at the water pail, at the time, and directed general attention to himself by strangling for several seconds and then squirting a slender thread of water over the blackboard.

Mr. Grimshaw fixed his eyes reproachfully on Charley, but said nothing. The real culprit (it wasn't Charley Marden, but the boy whose name I withhold) instantly regretted his badness, and after school confessed the whole thing to Mr. Grimshaw, who heaped coals of fire upon the nameless boy's head by giving him five cents for the Fourth of July. If Mr. Grimshaw had caned this unknown youth, the punishment would not have been half so severe.

On the last day of June, the Captain received a letter from my father, enclosing five dollars "for my son Tom," which enabled that young gentleman to make regal preparations for the celebration of our national independence. A portion of this money, two dollars, I hastened to invest in fireworks; the balance I put by for contingencies. In placing the fund in my possession, the Captain imposed one condition that dampened my ardor considerably—I was to buy no gunpowder. I might have all the snapping-crackers and torpedoes I wanted; but gunpowder was out of the question.

I thought this rather hard, for all my young friends were provided with pistols of various sizes. Pepper Whitcomb had a horse-pistol nearly as large as himself, and Jack Harris, though he to be sure was a big boy, was going to have a real old-fashioned flintlock musket. However, I didn't mean to let this drawback destroy my happiness. I had one charge of powder stowed away in the little brass pistol which I brought from New Orleans, and was bound to make a noise in the world once, if I never did again.

It was a custom observed from time immemorial for the town boys to have a bonfire on the Square on the midnight before the Fourth. I didn't ask the Captain's leave to attend this ceremony, for I had a general idea that he wouldn't give it. If the Captain, I reasoned, doesn't forbid me, I break no orders by going. Now this was a specious line of argument, and the mishaps that befell me in consequence of adopting it were richly deserved.

On the evening of the third I retired to bed very early, in order to disarm suspicion. I didn't sleep a wink, waiting for eleven o'clock to come round; and I thought it never would come round, as I lay counting from time to time the slow strokes of the ponderous bell in the steeple of the Old North Church. At length the laggard hour arrived. While the clock was striking I jumped out of bed and began dressing.

My grandfather and Miss Abigail were heavy sleepers, and I might have stolen downstairs and out at the front door undetected; but such a commonplace proceeding did not suit my adventurous disposition. I fastened one end of a rope (it was a few yards cut from Kitty Collins's clothesline) to the bedpost nearest the window, and cautiously climbed out on the wide pediment over the hall door. I had neglected to knot the rope; the result was, that, the moment I swung clear of the pediment, I descended like a flash of lightning, and warmed both my hands smartly. The rope moreover was four or five feet too short; so I got a fall that would have proved serious had I not tumbled into the middle of one of the big rosebushes growing on either side of the steps.

I scrambled out of that without delay, and was congratulating myself on my good luck, when I saw by the light of the setting moon the form of a man leaning over the garden gate. It was one of the town watch, who had probably been observing my operations with curiosity. Seeing no chance of escape, I put a bold face on the matter and walked directly up to him.

"What on airth air you a doin'?" asked the man, grasping the collar of my jacket.

"I live here, sir, if you please," I replied, "and am going to the bonfire. I didn't want to wake up the old folks, that's all."

The man cocked his eye at me in the most amiable manner, and released his hold.

"Boys is boys," he muttered. He didn't attempt to stop me as I slipped through the gate.

Once beyond his clutches, I took to my heels and soon reached the Square, where I found forty or fifty fellows assembled, engaged in building a pyramid of tar barrels. The palms of my hands still tingled so that I couldn't join in the sport. I stood in the doorway of the Nautilus Bank, watching the workers, among whom I recognized lots of my schoolmates. They looked like a legion of imps, coming and going in the twilight, busy in raising some

infernal edifice. What a Babel of voices it was, everybody directing everybody else, and everybody doing everything wrong!

When all was prepared, somebody applied a match to the somber pile. A fiery tongue thrust itself out here and there, then suddenly the whole fabric burst into flames, blazing and crackling beautifully. This was a signal for the boys to join hands and dance around the burning barrels, which they did shouting like mad creatures. When the fire had burnt down a little, fresh staves were brought and heaped on the pyre. In the excitement of the moment I forgot my tingling palms, and found myself in the thick of the carousal.

Before we were half ready, our combustible material was expended, and a disheartening kind of darkness settled down upon us. The boys collected together here and there in knots, consulting as to what should be done. It yet lacked four or five hours of daybreak, and none of us were in the humor to return to bed. I approached one of the groups standing near the town pump, and discovered in the uncertain light of the dying brands the figures of Jack Harris, Phil Adams, Harry Blake, and Pepper Whitcomb, their faces streaked with perspiration and tar, and their whole appearance suggestive of New Zealand chiefs.

"Hullo! here's Tom Bailey!" shouted Pepper Whitcomb; "he'll join in!"

Of course he would. The sting had gone out of my hands, and I was ripe for anything—none the less ripe for not knowing what was on the *tapis*. After whispering together for a moment, the boys motioned me to follow them.

We glided out from the crowd and silently wended our way through a neighboring alley, at the head of which stood a tumbledown old barn, owned by one Ezra Wingate. In former days this was the stable of the mail coach that ran between Rivermouth and Boston. When the railroad superseded that primitive mode of travel, the lumbering vehicle was rolled into the barn, and there it stayed. The stage driver, after prophesying the immediate downfall of the nation, died of grief and apoplexy, and the old coach followed in his wake as fast as it could by quietly dropping to pieces. The barn had the reputation of being haunted, and I think we all kept very close together when we found ourselves standing in the black shadow cast by the tall gable. Here, in a low voice, Jack Harris laid bare his plan, which was to burn the ancient stagecoach.

"The old trundle cart isn't worth twenty-five cents," said Jack Harris, "and Ezra Wingate ought to thank us for getting the rubbish out of the way. But if any fellow here doesn't want to have a hand in it, let him cut and run, and keep a quiet tongue in his head ever after."

With this he pulled out the staples that held the rusty padlock, and the big barn door swung slowly open. The interior of the stable was pitch dark, of course. As we made a movement to enter, a sudden scrambling, and the sound of heavy bodies leaping in all directions, caused us to start back in terror.

"Rats!" cried Phil Adams.

"Bats!" exclaimed Harry Blake.

"Cats!" suggested Jack Harris. "Who's afraid?"

Well, the truth is, we were all afraid; and if the pole of the stage had not been lying close to the threshold, I don't believe anything on earth would have induced us to cross it. We seized hold of the pole-straps and succeeded with great trouble in dragging the coach out. The two forewheels had rusted to the axle-tree, and refused to revolve. It was the merest skeleton of a coach. The cushions had long since been removed, and the leather hangings had crumbled away from the worm-eaten frame. A load of

ghosts and a span of phantom horses to drag them would
have made the ghastly thing complete.

Luckily for our undertaking, the stable stood at the
top of a very steep hill. With three boys to push behind,
and two in front to steer, we started the old coach on its
last trip with little or no difficulty. Our speed increased
every moment, and, the forewheels becoming unlocked as
we arrived at the foot of the declivity, we charged upon
the crowd like a regiment of cavalry, scattering the people
right and left. Before reaching the bonfire, to which some-
one had added several bushels of shavings, Jack Harris
and Phil Adams, who were steering, dropped on the
ground, and allowed the vehicle to pass over them, which
it did without injuring them; but the boys who were clinging for dear life to the trunk rack behind fell over the
prostrate steersmen, and there we all lay in a heap, two or
three of us quite picturesque with the nosebleed.

The coach, with an intuitive perception of what was
expected of it, plunged into the center of the kindling
shavings, and stopped. The flames sprung up and clung
to the rotten woodwork, which burned like tinder. At this
moment a figure was seen leaping wildly from the inside of
the blazing coach. The figure made three bounds towards
us, and tripped over Harry Blake. It was Pepper Whitcomb, with his hair somewhat singed, and his eyebrows
completely scorched off!

Pepper had slyly ensconced himself on the back seat
before we started, intending to have a neat little ride down
hill, and a laugh at us afterwards. But the laugh, as it
happened, was on our side, or would have been, if half a
dozen watchmen had not suddenly pounced down upon
us, as we lay scrambling on the ground, weak with our

mirth over Pepper's misfortune. We were collared and marched off before we well knew what had happened.

The abrupt transition from the noise and light of the Square to the silent, gloomy brick room in the rear of the Meat Market seemed like the work of enchantment. We stared at each other aghast.

"Well," remarked Jack Harris, with a sickly smile, "*this* is a go!"

"No go, I should say," whimpered Harry Blake, glancing at the bare brick walls and the heavy iron-plated door.

"Never say die," muttered Phil Adams, dolefully.

The bridewell was a small, low-studded chamber built up against the rear end of the Meat Market, and approached from the Square by a narrow passageway. A portion of the room was partitioned off into eight cells,

numbered, each capable of holding two persons. The cells
were full at the time, as we presently discovered by seeing
several hideous faces leering out at us through the gratings of the doors.

A smoky oil lamp in a lantern suspended from the ceiling threw a flickering light over the apartment, which
contained no furniture excepting a couple of stout
wooden benches. It was a dismal place by night, and only
little less dismal by day, for the tall houses surrounding
"the lock-up" prevented the faintest ray of sunshine from
penetrating the ventilator over the door—a long narrow
window opening inward and propped up by a piece of
lath.

As we seated ourselves in a row on one of the benches, I
imagine that our aspect was anything but cheerful.
Adams and Harris looked very anxious, and Harry Blake,
whose nose had just stopped bleeding, was mournfully
carving his name, by sheer force of habit, on the prison
bench. I don't think I ever saw a more "wrecked" expression on any human countenance than Pepper Whitcomb's
presented. His look of natural astonishment at finding
himself incarcerated in a jail was considerably heightened
by his lack of eyebrows. As for me, it was only by thinking
how the late Baron Trenck would have conducted himself under similar circumstances that I was able to re-
strain my tears.

None of us were inclined to conversation. A deep silence,
broken now and then by a startling snore from the cells,
reigned throughout the chamber. By and by, Pepper
Whitcomb glanced nervously towards Phil Adams and
said, "Phil, do you think they will—*hang us?*"

"Hang your grandmother!" returned Adams, impatiently; "what I'm afraid of is that they'll keep us locked up until the Fourth is over."

"You ain't smart ef they do!" cried a voice from one of the cells. It was a deep bass voice that sent a chill through me.

"Who are you?" said Jack Harris, addressing the cells in general; for the echoing qualities of the room made it difficult to locate the voice.

"That don't matter," replied the speaker, putting his face close up to the gratings of No. 3, "but ef I was a youngster like you, free an' easy outside there, with no bracelets * on, this spot wouldn't hold *me* long."

"That's so!" chimed several of the prison-birds, wagging their heads behind the iron lattices.

"Hush!" whispered Jack Harris, rising from his seat and walking on tiptoe to the door of cell No. 3. "What would you do?"

"Do? Why, I'd pile them 'ere benches up agin that 'ere door, an' crawl out of that 'ere winder in no time. That's my adwice."

"And wery good adwice it is, Jim," said the occupant of No. 5, approvingly.

Jack Harris seemed to be of the same opinion, for he hastily placed the benches one on the top of another under the ventilator, and, climbing up on the highest bench, peeped out into the passageway.

"If any gent happens to have a ninepence about him," said the man in cell No. 3, "there's a sufferin' family here as could make use of it. Smallest favors gratefully received, an' no questions axed."

This appeal touched a new silver quarter of a dollar in

* Handcuffs.

my trousers pocket; I fished out the coin from a mass of fireworks, and gave it to the prisoner. He appeared to be such a goodnatured fellow that I ventured to ask what he had done to get into jail.

"Intirely innocent. I was clapped in here by a rascally nevew as wishes to enjoy my wealth afore I'm dead."

"Your name, sir?" I inquired, with a view of reporting the outrage to my grandfather and having the injured person reinstated in society.

"Git out, you insolent young reptyle!" shouted the man, in a passion. I retreated precipitately, amid a roar of laughter from the other cells.

"Can't you keep still?" exclaimed Harris, withdrawing his head from the window.

A portly watchman usually sat on a stool outside the door day and night; but on this particular occasion, his services being required elsewhere, the bridewell had been left to guard itself.

"All clear," whispered Jack Harris, as he vanished through the aperture and dropped gently on the ground outside. We all followed him expeditiously—Pepper Whitcomb and myself getting stuck in the window for a moment in our frantic efforts not to be last.

"Now, boys, everybody for himself!"

THE ADVENTURES OF A FOURTH

THE sun cast a broad column of quivering gold across the river at the foot of our street, just as I reached the doorstep of the Nutter House. Kitty Collins, with her dress tucked about her so that she looked as if she had on a pair of calico trousers, was washing off the sidewalk.

"Arrah, you bad boy!" cried Kitty, leaning on the mop handle, "the Capen has jist been askin' for you. He's gone up town, now. It's a nate thing you done with my clothes-line, and it's me you may thank for gettin' it out of the way before the Capen come down."

The kind creature had hauled in the rope, and my escapade had not been discovered by the family; but I knew very well that the burning of the stagecoach, and the arrest of the boys concerned in the mischief, were sure to reach my grandfather's ears sooner or later.

"Well, Thomas," said the old gentleman, an hour or so afterwards, beaming upon me benevolently across the breakfast table, "you didn't wait to be called this morning."

"No, sir," I replied, growing very warm, "I took a little run up town to see what was going on."

75

I didn't say anything about the little run I took home again!

"They had quite a time on the Square last night," remarked Captain Nutter, looking up from the *Rivermouth Barnacle*, which was always placed beside his coffee cup at breakfast.

I felt that my hair was preparing to stand on end.

"Quite a time," continued my grandfather. "Some boys broke into Ezra Wingate's barn and carried off the old stagecoach. The young rascals! I do believe they'd burn up the whole town if they had their way."

With this he resumed the paper. After a long silence he exclaimed, "Hullo!"—upon which I nearly fell off the chair.

" 'Miscreants unknown,' " read my grandfather, following the paragraph with his forefinger; " 'escaped from the bridewell, leaving no clue to their identity, except the letter H, cut on one of the benches.' 'Five dollars reward offered for the apprehension of the perpetrators.' Sho! I hope Wingate will catch them."

I don't see how I continued to live, for on hearing this the breath went entirely out of my body. I beat a retreat from the room as soon as I could, and flew to the stable with a misty intention of mounting Gypsy and escaping from the place. I was pondering what steps to take, when Jack Harris and Charley Marden entered the yard.

"I say," said Harris, as blithe as a lark, "has old Wingate been here?"

"Been here?" I cried. "I should hope not!"

"The whole thing's out, you know," said Harris, pulling Gypsy's forelock over her eyes and blowing playfully into her nostrils.

"You don't mean it!" I gasped.

"Yes, I do, and we're to pay Wingate three dollars apiece. He'll make rather a good spec out of it."

"But how did he discover that we were the—the miscreants?" I asked, quoting mechanically from the *Rivermouth Barnacle*.

"Why, he saw us take the old ark, confound him! He's been trying to sell it any time these ten years. Now he has sold it to us. When he found that we had slipped out of the Meat Market, he went right off and wrote the advertisement offering five dollars reward; though he knew well enough who had taken the coach, for he came round to my father's house before the paper was printed to talk the matter over. Wasn't the governor mad, though! But it's all settled, I tell you. We're to pay Wingate fifteen dollars for the old go-cart, which he wanted to sell the other day for seventy-five cents, and couldn't. It's a downright swindle. But the funny part of it is to come."

"Oh, there's a funny part to it, is there?" I remarked bitterly.

"Yes. The moment Bill Conway saw the advertisement, he knew it was Harry Blake who cut that letter H on the bench; so off he rushes up to Wingate—kind of him, wasn't it?—and claims the reward. 'Too late, young man,' says old Wingate, 'the culprits has been discovered.' You see Sly-boots hadn't any intention of paying that five dollars."

Jack Harris's statement lifted a weight from my bosom. The article in the *Rivermouth Barnacle* had placed the affair before me in a new light. I had thoughtlessly committed a grave offense. Though the property in question was valueless, we were clearly wrong in destroying it. At the same time Mr. Wingate *had* tacitly sanctioned the act by not preventing it when he might easily have done so. He had allowed his property to be destroyed in order that he might realize a large profit.

Without waiting to hear more, I went straight to Captain Nutter, and, laying my remaining three dollars on his knee, confessed my share in the previous night's transaction.

The Captain heard me through in profound silence, pocketed the banknotes, and walked off without speaking a word. He had punished me in his own whimsical fashion at the breakfast table, for, at the very moment he was harrowing up my soul by reading the extracts from the *Rivermouth Barnacle*, he not only knew all about the bonfire, but had paid Ezra Wingate his three dollars. Such was the duplicity of that aged impostor!

I think Captain Nutter was justified in retaining my pocket money, as additional punishment, though the possession of it later in the day would have got me out of a difficult position, as the reader will see further on.

I returned with a light heart and a large piece of punk to my friends in the stableyard, where we celebrated the termination of our trouble by setting off two packs of firecrackers in an empty wine cask. They made a prodigious racket, but failed somehow to fully express my feelings. The little brass pistol in my bedroom suddenly occurred to me. It had been loaded I don't know how many months, long before I left New Orleans, and now was the time, if ever, to fire it off. Muskets, blunderbusses, and pistols were banging away lively all over town, and the smell of gunpowder, floating on the air, set me wild to add something respectable to the universal din.

When the pistol was produced, Jack Harris examined the rusty cap and prophesied that it would not explode. "Never mind," said I, "let's try it."

I had fired the pistol once, secretly, in New Orleans, and, remembering the noise it gave birth to on that occasion, I shut both eyes tight as I pulled the trigger. The hammer clicked on the cap with a dull, dead sound. Then

Harris tried it; then Charley Marden; then I took it again, and after three or four trials was on the point of giving it up as a bad job, when the obstinate thing went off with a tremendous explosion, nearly jerking my arm from the socket. The smoke cleared away, and there I stood with the stock of the pistol clutched convulsively in my hand—the barrel, lock, trigger, and ramrod having vanished into thin air.

"Are you hurt?" cried the boys, in one breath.

"N—no," I replied, dubiously, for the concussion had bewildered me a little.

When I realized the nature of the calamity, my grief was excessive. I can't imagine what led me to do so ridiculous a thing, but I gravely buried the remains of my beloved pistol in our back garden, and erected over the mound a slate tablet to the effect that "Mr. Barker, formerly of New Orleans, was killed accidentally on the Fourth of July, 18— in the 2nd year of his Age." * Binny Wallace, arriving on the spot just after the disaster, and Charley Marden (who enjoyed the obsequies immensely), acted with me as chief mourners. I, for my part, was a very sincere one.

As I turned away in a disconsolate mood from the garden, Charley Marden remarked that he shouldn't be surprised if the pistol butt took root and grew into a mahogany tree or something. He said he once planted an old musket stock, and shortly afterwards a lot of *shoots* sprung up! Jack Harris laughed; but neither I nor Binny Wallace saw Charley's wicked joke.

We were now joined by Pepper Whitcomb, Fred Langdon, and several other desperate characters, on their way to the Square, which was always a busy place when public festivities were going on. Feeling that I was still in disgrace with the Captain, I thought it politic to ask his consent before accompanying the boys. He gave it with some hesitation, advising me to be careful not to get in front of the firearms. Once he put his fingers mechanically into his vest pocket and half drew forth some dollar bills, then slowly thrust them back again as his sense of justice overcame his genial disposition. I guess it cut the old gentleman to the heart to be obliged to keep me out of my pocket money. I know it did me. However, as I was

---

* This inscription is copied from a triangular-shaped piece of slate, still preserved in the garret of the Nutter House, together with the pistol butt itself, which was subsequently dug up for a post-mortem examination.

passing through the hall, Miss Abigail, with a very severe cast of countenance, slipped a brand-new quarter into my hand. We had silver currency in those days, thank Heaven!

Great were the bustle and confusion on the Square. By the way, I don't know why they called this large open space a square, unless because it was an oval—an oval formed by the confluence of half a dozen streets, now thronged by crowds of smartly dressed townspeople and country folks; for Rivermouth on the Fourth was the center of attraction to the inhabitants of the neighboring villages.

On one side of the Square were twenty or thirty booths arranged in a semicircle, gay with little flags, and seductive with lemonade, ginger beer, and seed cakes. Here and there were tables at which could be purchased the smaller sort of fireworks, such as pinwheels, serpents, double headers, and punk warranted not to go out. Many of the adjacent houses made a pretty display of bunting, and across each of the streets opening on the Square was an arch of spruce and evergreen, blossoming all over with patriotic mottoes and paper roses.

It was a noisy, merry, bewildering scene as we came upon the ground. The incessant rattle of small arms, the booming of the twelve-pounder firing on the Mill Dam, and the silvery clangor of the church bells ringing simultaneously—not to mention an ambitious brass band that was blowing itself to pieces on a balcony—were enough to drive one distracted. We amused ourselves for an hour or two, darting in and out among the crowd and setting off our crackers. At one o'clock the Hon. Hezekiah Elkins mounted a platform in the middle of the Square and delivered an oration, to which his fellow citizens didn't pay much attention, having all they could do to dodge the squibs that were set loose upon them by mischievous boys stationed on the surrounding housetops.

Our little party, which had picked up recruits here and there, not being swayed by eloquence, withdrew to a booth on the outskirts of the crowd, where we regaled ourselves with root beer at two cents a glass. I recollect being much struck by the placard surmounting this tent:

ROOT BEER
SOLD HERE.

It seemed to me the perfection of pith and poetry. What could be more terse? Not a word to spare, and yet everything fully expressed. Rhyme and rhythm faultless. It was a delightful poet who made those verses. As for the beer itself—that, I think, must have been made from the root of all evil! A single glass of it insured an uninterrupted pain for twenty-four hours. The influence of my liberality working on Charley Marden—for it was I who paid for the beer—he presently invited us all to take an ice cream with him at Pettingil's saloon. Pettingil was the Delmonico of Rivermouth. He furnished ices and confectionery for aristocratic balls and parties, and didn't disdain to officiate as leader of the orchestra at the same; for Pettingil played on the violin, as Pepper Whitcomb described it, "like Old Scratch."

Pettingil's confectionery store was on the corner of Willow and High Streets. The saloon, separated from the shop by a flight of three steps leading to a door hung

with faded red drapery, had about it an air of mystery
and seclusion quite delightful. Four windows, also draped,
faced the side street, affording an unobstructed view of
Marm Hatch's back yard, where a number of inexplicable
garments on a clothesline were always to be seen careering
in the wind.

There was a lull just then in the ice-cream business, it
being dinner time, and we found the saloon unoccupied.
When we had seated ourselves around the largest marble-
topped table, Charley Marden in a manly voice ordered
twelve sixpenny ice creams, "strawberry and verneller
mixed."

It was a magnificent sight, those twelve chilly glasses
entering the room on a waiter, the red and white custard
rising from each glass like a church steeple, and the spoon
handle shooting up from the apex like a spire. I doubt
if a person of the nicest palate could have distinguished,
with his eyes shut, which was the vanilla and which the
strawberry; but, if I could at this moment obtain a cream
tasting as that did, I would give five dollars for a very
small quantity.

We fell to with a will, and so evenly balanced were our
capabilities that we finished our creams together, the
spoons clinking in the glasses like one spoon.

"Let's have some more!" cried Charley Marden, with
the air of Aladdin ordering up a fresh hogshead of pearls
and rubies. "Tom Bailey, tell Pettingil to send in another
round."

Could I credit my ears? I looked at him to see if he
were in earnest. He meant it. In a moment more I was
leaning over the counter giving directions for a second
supply. Thinking it would make no difference to such a

gorgeous young sybarite as Marden, I took the liberty of ordering ninepenny creams this time.

On returning to the saloon, what was my horror at finding it empty!

There were the twelve cloudy glasses, standing in a circle on the sticky marble slab, and not a boy to be seen.

A pair of hands letting go their hold on the windowsill outside explained matters. I had been made a victim.

I couldn't stay and face Pettingil, whose peppery temper was well known among the boys. I hadn't a cent in the world to appease him. What should I do? I heard the clink of approaching glasses—the ninepenny creams. I rushed to the nearest window. It was only five feet to the ground. I threw myself out as if I had been an old hat.

Landing on my feet, I fled breathlessly down High Street, through Willow, and was turning into Brierwood Place when the sound of several voices, calling to me in distress, stopped my progress.

"Look out, you fool! the mine! the mine!" yelled the warning voices.

Several men and boys were standing at the head of the street, making insane gestures to me to avoid something. But I saw no mine, only in the middle of the road in front of me was a common flour barrel, which, as I gazed at it, suddenly rose into the air with a terrific explosion. I felt myself thrown violently off my feet. I remember nothing else, excepting that, as I went up, I caught a momentary glimpse of Ezra Wingate leering through his shop window like an avenging spirit.

For an account of what followed, I am indebted to hearsay, for I was insensible when the people picked me up and carried me home on a shutter borrowed from the proprietor of Pettingil's saloon. I was supposed to be killed, but happily (happily for me, at least) I was merely stunned. I lay in a semi-unconscious state until eight o'clock that night, when I attempted to speak. Miss Abigail, who watched by the bedside, put her ear down to my lips and was saluted with these remarkable words:—

"Root Beer
Sold Here!"

I BECOME AN R. M. C.

IN THE course of ten days I recovered sufficiently
from my injuries to attend school, where, for a little
while, I was looked upon as a hero, on account of having
been blown up. What don't we make a hero of? The distraction which prevailed in the classes the week preceding
the Fourth had subsided, and nothing remained to indi-
cate the recent festivities, excepting a noticeable want
of eyebrows on the part of Pepper Whitcomb and myself.

In August we had two weeks' vacation. It was about
this time that I became a member of the Rivermouth
Centipedes, a secret society composed of twelve of the
Temple Grammar School boys. This was an honor to
which I had long aspired, but, being a new boy, I was not
admitted to the fraternity until my character had fully
developed itself.

It was a very select society, the object of which I never
fathomed, though I was an active member of the body
during the remainder of my residence at Rivermouth, and
at one time held the onerous position of F. C.—First Centipede. Each of the elect wore a copper cent (some occult
association being established between a cent apiece and

86

a centipede!) suspended by a string round his neck. The medals were worn next the skin, and it was while bathing one day at Grave Point, with Jack Harris and Fred Langdon, that I had my curiosity roused to the highest pitch by a sight of these singular emblems. As soon as I ascertained the existence of a boys' club, of course I was ready to die to join it. And eventually I was allowed to join.

The initiation ceremony took place in Fred Langdon's barn, where I was submitted to a series of trials not calculated to soothe the nerves of a timorous boy. Before being led to the Grotto of Enchantment—such was the modest title given to the loft over my friend's woodhouse —my hands were securely pinioned, and my eyes covered with a thick silk handkerchief. At the head of the stairs, I was told in an unrecognizable, husky voice, that it was not yet too late to retreat if I felt myself physically too weak to undergo the necessary tortures. I replied that I was not too weak, in a tone which I intended to be resolute, but which, in spite of me, seemed to come from the pit of my stomach.

"It is well!" said the husky voice.

I did not feel so sure about that; but, having made up my mind to be a Centipede, a Centipede I was bound to be. Other boys had passed through the ordeal and lived, why should not I?

A prolonged silence followed this preliminary examination, and I was wondering what would come next, when a pistol fired off close by my ear deafened me for a moment. The unknown voice then directed me to take ten steps forward and stop at the word halt. I took ten steps, and halted.

"Stricken mortal," said a second husky voice, more husky, if possible, than the first, "if you had advanced another inch, you would have disappeared down an abyss three thousand feet deep!"

I naturally shrunk back at this friendly piece of information. A prick from some two-pronged instrument, evidently a pitchfork, gently checked my retreat. I was then conducted to the brink of several other precipices, and ordered to step over many dangerous chasms, where the result would have been instant death if I had committed the least mistake. I have neglected to say that my movements were accompanied by dismal groans from the various parts of the grotto.

Finally, I was led up a steep plank to what appeared to me an incalculable height. Here I stood breathless while the by-laws were read aloud. A more extraordinary code of laws never came from the brain of man. The penalties attached to the abject being who should reveal any of the secrets of the society were enough to make the blood run cold. A second pistol shot was heard, the something I stood on sunk with a crash beneath my feet, and I fell two miles, as nearly as I could compute it. At the same instant the handkerchief was whisked from my eyes, and I found myself standing in an empty hogshead surrounded by twelve masked figures fantastically dressed. One of the conspirators was really appalling with a tin saucepan on his head, and a tigerskin sleigh robe thrown over his shoulders. I scarcely need say that there were no vestiges to be seen of the fearful gulfs over which I had passed so cautiously. My ascent had been to the top of the hogshead, and my descent to the bottom thereof. Holding one another by the hand, and chanting a low dirge, the Mystic Twelve revolved about me. This concluded the ceremony. With a merry shout the boys threw off their masks, and I was declared a regularly installed member of the R. M. C.

I afterwards had a good deal of sport out of the club, for these initiations, as you can imagine, were sometimes very comical spectacles, especially when the aspirant for centipedal honors happened to be of a timid disposition. If he showed the slightest terror, he was certain to be tricked unmercifully. One of our subsequent devices— a humble invention of my own—was to request the candidate to put out his tongue, whereupon the First Centipede would say, in a low tone, as if not intended for the ear of the victim, "Diabolus, fetch me the red-hot iron!" The expedition with which that tongue would disappear was simply ridiculous.

Our meetings were held in various barns, at no stated periods, but as circumstances suggested. Any member had a right to call a meeting. Each boy who failed to report himself was fined one cent. Whenever a member had reasons for thinking that another member would be unable to attend, he called a meeting. For instance, immediately on learning the death of Harry Blake's great-grandfather, I issued a call. By these simple and ingenious measures we kept our treasury in a flourishing condition, sometimes having on hand as much as a dollar and a quarter.

I have said that the society had no especial object. It is true, there was a tacit understanding among us that the Centipedes were to stand by one another on all occasions, though I don't remember that they did; but further than this we had no purpose, unless it was to accomplish as a body the same amount of mischief which we were sure to do as individuals. To mystify the staid and slow-going Rivermouthians was our frequent pleasure. Several of our pranks won us such a reputation among the towns-folk, that we were credited with having a large finger in whatever went amiss in the place.

One morning about a week after my admission into the secret order, the quiet citizens awoke to find that the signboards of all the principal streets had changed places during the night. People who went trustfully to sleep in Currant Square opened their eyes in Honeysuckle Terrace. Jones's Avenue at the north end had suddenly become Walnut Street, and Peanut Street was nowhere to be found. Confusion reigned. The town authorities took the matter in hand without delay, and six of the Temple Grammar School boys were summoned to appear before Justice Clapham.

Having tearfully disclaimed to my grandfather all knowledge of the transaction, I disappeared from the family circle, and was not apprehended until late in the afternoon, when the Captain dragged me ignominiously from the hay mow and conducted me, more dead than alive, to the office of Justice Clapham. Here I encountered five other pallid culprits, who had been fished out of divers coalbins, garrets, and chickencoops, to answer the demands of the outraged laws. (Charley Marden had hidden himself in a pile of gravel behind his father's house, and looked like a recently exhumed mummy.)

There was not a particle of evidence against us; and, indeed, we were wholly innocent of the offense. The trick, as was afterwards proved, had been played by a party of soldiers stationed at the fort in the harbor. We were indebted for our arrest to Master Conway, who had slyly dropped a hint, within the hearing of Selectman Mudge, to the effect that "young Bailey and his five cronies could tell something about them signs." When he was called upon to make good his assertion, he was considerably more terrified than the Centipedes, though *they* were ready to sink into their shoes.

At our next meeting, it was unanimously resolved that Conway's animosity should not be quietly submitted to. He had sought to inform against us in the stage-coach business; he had volunteered to carry Pettingil's "little bill" for twenty-four ice creams to Charley Marden's father; and now he had caused us to be arraigned before Justice Clapham on a charge equally groundless and painful. After much noisy discussion a plan of retaliation was agreed upon.

There was a certain slim, mild apothecary in the town, by the name of Meeks. It was generally given out that Mr. Meeks had a vague desire to get married, but, being a shy and timorous youth, lacked the moral courage to do so. It was also well known that the widow Conway had not buried her heart with the late lamented. As to her shyness, that was not so clear. Indeed, her attentions to Mr. Meeks, whose mother she might have been, were of a nature not to be misunderstood, and were not misunderstood by any one but Mr. Meeks himself.

The widow carried on a dressmaking establishment at her residence on the corner opposite Meeks's drugstore, and kept a wary eye on all the young ladies from Miss Dorothy Gibbs's Female Institute who patronized the shop for soda water, acid drops, and slate pencils. In the afternoon the widow was usually seen seated, smartly dressed, at her window upstairs, casting destructive glances across the street—the artificial roses in her cap and her whole languishing manner saying as plainly as a label on a prescription, "To Be Taken Immediately!" But Mr. Meeks didn't take.

The lady's fondness, and the gentleman's blindness, were topics ably handled at every sewing circle in the town. It was through these two luckless individuals that we proposed to strike a deadly blow at the common enemy. To kill less than three birds with one stone, did not suit our sanguinary purpose. We disliked the widow not so much for her sentimentality as for being the mother of Bill Conway; we disliked Mr. Meeks, not because he was insipid, like his own sirups, but because the widow loved him; Bill Conway we hated for himself.

Late one dark Saturday night in September,

we carried our plan into effect. On the following morning, as the orderly citizens wended their way to church past the widow's abode, their sober faces relaxed at beholding over her front door the well-known gilt Mortar and Pestle which usually stood on the top of a pole on the opposite corner; while the passers on that side of the street were equally amused and scandalized at seeing a placard bearing the following announcement tacked to the druggist's window-shutters:

Wanted, a Sempstress!

The naughty cleverness of the joke (which I should be sorry to defend) was recognized at once. It spread like wildfire over the town, and, though the mortar and the placard were speedily removed, our triumph was complete. The whole community was on the broad grin, and our participation in the affair seemingly unsuspected. It was those wicked soldiers at the Fort!

❋ T E N ❋

I FIGHT CONWAY

THERE was one person, however, who cherished a strong suspicion that the Centipedes had had a hand in the business; and that person was Conway. His red hair seemed to change to a livelier red, and his sallow cheeks to a deeper sallow, as we glanced at him stealthily over the tops of our slates the next day in school. He knew we were watching him, and made sundry mouths and scowled in the most threatening way over his sums.

Conway had an accomplishment peculiarly his own— that of throwing his thumbs out of joint at will. Sometimes while absorbed in study, or on becoming nervous at recitation, he performed the feat unconsciously. Throughout this entire morning, his thumbs were observed to be in a chronic state of dislocation, indicating great mental agitation on the part of the owner. We fully expected an outbreak from him at recess; but the intermission passed off tranquilly, somewhat to our disappointment.

At the close of the afternoon session, it happened that Binny Wallace and myself, having got swamped in our

94

Latin exercise, were detained in school for the purpose of refreshing our memories with a page of Mr. Andrews's perplexingly irregular verbs. Binny Wallace, finishing his task first, was dismissed. I followed shortly after, and, on stepping into the playground, saw my little friend plastered, as it were, up against the fence, and Conway standing in front of him ready to deliver a blow on the upturned, unprotected face, whose gentleness would have stayed any arm but a coward's.

Seth Rodgers, with both hands in his pockets, was leaning against the pump lazily enjoying the sport; but on seeing me sweep across the yard, whirling my strap of books in the air like a sling, he called out lustily, "Lay low, Conway! here's young Bailey!"

Conway turned just in time to catch on his shoulder the blow intended for his head. He reached forward one of his long arms—he had arms like a windmill, that boy —and, grasping me by the hair, tore out quite a respectable handful. The tears flew to my eyes, but they were not tears of pain; they were merely the involuntary tribute which nature paid to the departed tresses.

In a second my little jacket lay on the ground, and I stood on guard, resting lightly on my right leg and keeping my eye fixed steadily on Conway's—in all of which I was faithfully following the instructions of Phil Adams, whose father subscribed to a sporting journal.

Conway also threw himself into a defensive attitude, and there we were, glaring at each other, motionless, neither of us disposed to risk an attack, but both on the alert to resist one. There is no telling how long we might have remained in that absurd position, had we not been interrupted.

It was a custom with the larger pupils to return to the playground after school, and play baseball until sundown. The town authorities had prohibited ball-playing on the Square, and, there being no other available place, the boys fell back perforce on the school yard. Just at this crisis, a dozen or so of the Templars entered the gate, and, seeing at a glance the belligerent status of Conway and myself, dropped bat and ball, and rushed to the spot where we stood.

"Is it a fight?" asked Phil Adams, who saw by our freshness that we had not yet got to work.

"Yes, it's a fight," I answered, "unless Conway will ask Wallace's pardon, promise never to hector me in future—and put back my hair!"

This last condition was rather a staggerer.

"I sha'n't do nothing of the sort," said Conway, sulkily.

"Then the thing must go on," said Adams, with dignity. "Rodgers, as I understand it, is your second, Conway? Bailey, come here. What's the row about?"

"He was thrashing Binny Wallace."

"No, I wasn't," interrupted Conway; "but I was going to, because he knows who put Meeks's mortar over our door. And I know well enough who did it; it was that sneaking little mulatter!"—pointing at me.

"O, by George!" I cried, reddening at the insult.

"Cool is the word," said Adams, as he bound a handkerchief round my head, and carefully tucked away the long straggling locks that offered a tempting advantage to the enemy. "Who ever heard of a fellow with such a head of hair going into action!" muttered Phil, twitching the handkerchief to ascertain if it were securely tied. He then loosened my galluses (braces), and buckled them tightly above my hips. "Now, then, bantam, never say die!"

Conway regarded these business-like preparations with evident misgiving, for he called Rodgers to his side, and had himself arrayed in a similar manner, though his hair was cropped so close that you couldn't have taken hold of it with a pair of tweezers.

"Is your man ready?" asked Phil Adams, addressing Rodgers.

"Ready!"

"Keep your back to the gate, Tom," whispered Phil in my ear, "and you'll have the sun in his eyes."

Behold us once more face to face, like David and the Philistine. Look at us as long as you may; for this is all you shall see of the combat. According to my thinking, the hospital teaches a better lesson than the battlefield. I will tell you about my black eye, and my swollen lip, if you will; but not a word of the fight.

You'll get no description of it from me, simply because

I think it would prove very poor reading, and not because I consider my revolt against Conway's tyranny unjustifiable.

I had borne Conway's persecutions for many months with lamb-like patience. I might have shielded myself by appealing to Mr. Grimshaw; but no boy in the Temple Grammar School could do that without losing caste. Whether this was just or not, doesn't matter a pin, since it was so—a traditionary law of the place. The personal inconvenience I suffered from my tormentor was nothing to the pain he inflicted on me indirectly by his persistent cruelty to little Binny Wallace. I should have lacked the spirit of a hen if I had not resented it finally. I am glad that I faced Conway, and asked no favors, and got rid of him forever. I am glad that Phil Adams taught me to box, and I say to all youngsters: Learn to box, to ride, to pull an oar, and to swim. The occasion may come round, when a decent proficiency in one or the rest of these accomplishments will be of service to you.

In one of the best books * ever written for boys are these words:

"Learn to box, then, as you learn to play cricket and football. Not one of you will be the worse, but very much the better, for learning to box well. Should you never have to use it in earnest, there's no exercise in the world so good for the temper, and for the muscles of the back and legs.

"As for fighting, keep out of it, if you can, by all means. When the time comes, if ever it should, that you have to say 'Yes' or 'No' to a challenge to fight, say 'No' if you can—only take care you make it plain to yourself why

* *Tom Brown's School Days at Rugby.*

you say 'No.' It's a proof of the highest courage, if done from true Christian motives. It's quite right and justifiable, if done from a simple aversion to physical pain and danger. But don't say 'No' because you fear a licking and say or think it's because you fear God, for that's neither Christian nor honest. And if you do fight, fight it out; and don't give in while you can stand and see."

And don't give in when you can't! say I. For I could stand very little, and see not at all (having pummeled the school pump for the last twenty seconds), when Conway retired from the field. As Phil Adams stepped up to shake hands with me, he received a telling blow in the stomach; for all the fight was not out of me yet, and I mistook him for a new adversary.

Convinced of my error, I accepted his congratulations, with those of the other boys, blandly and blindly. I remember that Binny Wallace wanted to give me his silver pencil-case. The gentle soul had stood throughout the contest with his face turned to the fence, suffering untold agony.

A good wash at the pump, and a cold key applied to my eye, refreshed me amazingly. Escorted by two or three of the schoolfellows, I walked home through the pleasant autumn twilight, battered but triumphant. As I went along, my cap cocked on one side to keep the chilly air from my eye, I felt that I was not only following my nose, but following it so closely, that I was in some danger of treading on it. I seemed to have nose enough for the whole party. My left cheek, also, was puffed out like a dumpling. I couldn't help saying to myself, "If *this* is victory, how about that other fellow?"

"Tom," said Harry Blake, hesitating.

"Well?"

"Did you see Mr. Grimshaw looking out of the recitation-room window just as we left the yard?"

"No; was he, though?"

"I am sure of it."

"Then he must have seen all the row."

"Shouldn't wonder."

"No, he didn't," broke in Adams, "or he would have stopped it short meter; but I guess he saw you pitching into the pump—which you did uncommonly strong—and of course he smelt mischief directly."

"Well, it can't be helped now," I reflected.

"—As the monkey said when he fell out of the cocoanut tree," added Charley Marden, trying to make me laugh.

It was early candlelight when we reached the house. Miss Abigail, opening the front door, started back at my hilarious appearance. I tried to smile upon her sweetly, but the smile, rippling over my swollen cheek, and dying away like a spent wave on my nose, produced an expression of which Miss Abigail declared she had never seen the like excepting on the face of a Chinese idol.

She hustled me unceremoniously into the presence of my grandfather in the sitting-room. Captain Nutter, as the recognized professional warrior of our family, could not consistently take me to task for fighting Conway; nor was he disposed to do so; for the Captain was well aware of the long-continued provocation I had endured.

"Ah, you rascal!" cried the old gentleman, after hearing my story, "just like me when I was young—always in one kind of trouble or another. I believe it runs in the family."

"I think," said Miss Abigail, without the faintest expression on her countenance, "that a tablespoonful of hot dro—"

The Captain interrupted Miss Abigail peremptorily, directing her to make a shade out of cardboard and black silk, to tie over my eye. Miss Abigail must have been possessed with the idea that I had taken up pugilism as a profession, for she turned out no fewer than six of these blinders.

"They'll be handy to have in the house," says Miss Abigail, grimly.

Of course, so great a breach of discipline was not to be passed over by Mr. Grimshaw. He had, as we suspected, witnessed the closing scene of the fight from the schoolroom window, and the next morning, after prayers, I was not wholly unprepared when Master Conway and myself were called up to the desk for examination. Conway, with a piece of court plaster in the shape of a Maltese cross on his right cheek, and I with the silk patch over my left eye, caused a general titter through the room.

"Silence!" said Mr. Grimshaw, sharply.

As the reader is already familiar with the leading points in the case of Bailey versus Conway, I shall not report the trial further than to say that Adams, Marden, and several other pupils testified to the fact that Conway had imposed on me ever since my first day at the Temple School. Their evidence also went to show that Conway was a quarrelsome character generally. Bad for Conway. Seth Rodgers, on the part of his friend, proved that I had struck the first blow. That was bad for me.

"If you please, sir," said Binny Wallace, holding up his hand for permission to speak, "Bailey didn't fight on his own account; he fought on my account, and, if you please, sir, I am the boy to be blamed, for I was the cause of the trouble."

This drew out the story of Conway's harsh treatment of the smaller boys. As Binny related the wrongs of his playfellows, saying very little of his own grievances, I noticed that Mr. Grimshaw's hand, unknown to himself perhaps, rested lightly from time to time on Wallace's sunny hair. The examination finished, Mr. Grimshaw leaned on the desk thoughtfully for a moment, and then said:

"Every boy in this school knows that it is against the rules to fight. If one boy maltreats another, within school bounds, or within school hours, that is a matter for me to settle. The case should be laid before me. I disapprove of tale bearing, I never encourage it in the slightest degree; but when one pupil systematically persecutes a schoolmate, it is the duty of some head boy to inform me. No pupil has a right to take the law into his own hands. If there is any fighting to be done, I am the proper person to do it. I disapprove of boys' fighting; it is unnecessary and unchristian. In the present instance, I consider every large boy in this school at fault; but as the offense is one of omission, rather than commission, my punishment must rest only on the two boys convicted of misdemeanor. Conway loses his recess for a month, and Bailey has a page added to his Latin lessons for the next four recitations. I now request Bailey and Conway to shake hands in the presence of the school, and acknowledge their regret at what has occurred."

Conway and I approached each other slowly and cautiously, as if we were bent upon another hostile collision.

We clasped hands in the tamest manner imaginable, and Conway mumbled, "I'm sorry I fought with you."

"I think you are," I replied, dryly, "and I'm sorry I had to thrash you."

"You can go to your seats," said Mr. Grimshaw, turning his face aside to hide a smile. I am sure my apology was a very good one.

I never had any more trouble with Conway. He and his shadow, Seth Rodgers, gave me a wide berth for many months. Nor was Binny Wal- lace subjected to further molestation. Miss Abigail's sanitary stores, including a bottle of opodeldoc, were never called into requisition. The six black silk patches, with their elastic strings, are still dangling from a beam in the garret of the Nutter House, waiting for me to get into fresh difficulties.

ELEVEN

ALL ABOUT GYPSY

THIS record of my life at Rivermouth would be
strangely incomplete did I not devote an entire
chapter to Gypsy. I had other pets, of course; for what
healthy boy could long exist without numerous friends in
the animal kingdom? I had two white mice that were forever gnawing their way out of a pasteboard *château*, and
crawling over my face when I lay asleep. I used to keep
the pink-eyed little beggars in my bedroom, greatly to
the annoyance of Miss Abigail, who was constantly fancy-
ing that one of the mice had secreted itself somewhere
about her person.

I also owned a dog, a terrier, who managed in some in-
scrutable way to pick a quarrel with the moon, and on
bright nights kept up such a ki-yi-ing in our back garden,
that we were finally forced to dispose of him at private

sale. He was purchased by Mr. Oxford, the butcher. I protested against the arrangement, and ever afterwards, when we had sausages from Mr. Oxford's shop, I made believe I detected in them certain evidences that Cato had been foully dealt with.

Of birds I had no end—robins, purple martins, wrens, bulfinches, bobolinks, ring doves, and pigeons. At one time I took solid comfort in the iniquitous society of a dissipated old parrot, who talked so terribly, that the Rev. Wibird Hawkins, happening to get a sample of Poll's vituperative powers, pronounced him "a benighted heathen," and advised the Captain to get rid of him. A brace of turtles supplanted the parrot in my affections; the turtles gave way to rabbits; and the rabbits in turn yielded to the superior charms of a small monkey, which the Captain bought of a sailor lately from the coast of Africa.

But Gypsy was the prime favorite, in spite of many rivals. I never grew weary of her. She was the most knowing little thing in the world. Her proper sphere in life—and the one to which she ultimately attained—was the sawdust arena of a traveling circus. There was nothing short of the three R's, reading, 'riting, and 'rithmetic, that Gypsy couldn't be taught. The gift of speech was not hers, but the faculty of thought was. She combined the wisdom of the serpent with the harmlessness of the dove.

My little friend, to be sure, was not exempt from certain graceful weaknesses, inseparable, perhaps, from the female character. She was very pretty—and she knew it. She was also passionately fond of dress—by which I mean her best harness. When she had this on, her curvetings and prancings were laughable, though in ordinary tackle

she went along demurely enough. There was something in
the enameled leather and the silver-washed mountings that
chimed with her artistic sense. To have her mane braided,
and a rose or a pansy stuck into her forelock, was to make
her too conceited for anything.

She had another trait not rare among her sex. She liked
the attentions of young gentlemen, while the society of
girls bored her. She would drag them, sulkily, in the cart;
but as for permitting one of them in the saddle, the idea
was preposterous. Once when Pepper Whitcomb's sister,
in spite of our remonstrances, ventured to mount her,
Gypsy gave a little indignant neigh, and tossed the gentle
Emma heels over head in no time. But with any of the
boys the mare was as docile as a lamb.

Her treatment of the several members of the family was
comical. For the Captain she entertained a wholesome respect, and was always on her good behavior when he was
around. As to Miss Abigail, Gypsy simply laughed at *her*
—literally laughed, contracting her upper lip and dis-
playing all her snow-white teeth, as if something about
Miss Abigail struck her, Gypsy, as being extremely ridiculous.

Kitty Collins, for some reason or another, was afraid of
the pony, or pretended to be. The sagacious little animal
knew it, of course, and frequently, when Kitty was hanging out clothes near the stable, the mare, being loose in
the yard, would make short plunges at her. Once Gypsy
seized the basket of clothespins with her teeth, and rising
on her hind legs, pawing the air with her fore feet, followed Kitty clear up to the scullery steps.

That part of the yard was shut off from the rest by a
gate; but no gate was proof against Gypsy's ingenuity.

She could let down bars, lift up latches, draw bolts, and
turn all sorts of buttons. This accomplishment rendered
it hazardous for Miss Abigail or Kitty to leave any eatables on the kitchen table near the window. On one occasion Gypsy put in her head and lapped up six custard
pies that had been placed by the casement to cool.

An account of my young lady's various pranks would
fill a thick volume. A favorite trick of hers, on being requested to "walk like Miss Abigail," was to assume a little
skittish gait so true to nature that Miss Abigail herself
was obliged to admit the cleverness of the imitation.

The idea of putting Gypsy through a systematic course
of instruction was suggested to me by a visit to the circus
which gave an annual performance in Rivermouth. This
show embraced, among its attractions, a number of trained
Shetland ponies, and I determined that Gypsy should
likewise have the benefit of a liberal education. I succeeded in teaching her to waltz, to fire a pistol by tugging
at a string tied to the trigger, to lie down dead, to wink

one eye, and to execute many other feats of a difficult nature. She took to her studies admirably, and enjoyed the whole thing as much as anybody.

The monkey was a perpetual marvel to Gypsy. They became bosom friends in an incredibly brief period, and were never easy out of each other's sight. Prince Zany— that's what Pepper Whitcomb and I christened him one day, much to the disgust of the monkey, who bit a piece out of Pepper's nose—resided in the stable, and went to roost every night on the pony's back, where I usually found him in the morning. Whenever I rode out, I was obliged to secure His Highness the Prince with a stout cord to the fence, he chattering all the time like a madman.

One afternoon as I was cantering through the crowded part of the town, I noticed that the people in the street stopped, stared at me, and fell to laughing. I turned round in the saddle, and there was Zany, with a great burdock leaf in his paw, perched up behind me on the crupper, as solemn as a judge.

After a few months, poor Zany sickened mysteriously, and died. The dark thought occurred to me then, and comes back to me now with redoubled force, that Miss Abigail must have given him some hot drops. Zany left a large circle of sorrowing friends, if not relatives. Gypsy, I think, never entirely recovered from the shock occasioned by his early demise. She became fonder of me, though; and one of her cunningest demonstrations was to escape from the stable yard, and trot up to the door of the Temple Grammar School, where I would discover her at recess patiently waiting for me, with her fore feet on the second step, and wisps of straw standing out all over her.

I should fail if I tried to tell you how dear the pony was to me. Even hard, unloving men become attached to the horses they take care of; so I, who was neither unloving nor hard, grew to love every glossy hair of the pretty little creature that depended on me for her soft straw bed and her daily modicum of oats. In my prayer at night I never forgot to mention Gypsy with the rest of the family— generally setting forth her claims first.

Whatever relates to Gypsy belongs properly to this narrative; therefore I offer no apology for rescuing from oblivion, and boldly printing here, a short composition which I wrote in the early part of my first quarter at the Temple Grammar School. It is my maiden effort in a difficult art, and is, perhaps, lacking in those graces of thought and style which are reached only after the severest practice.

Every Wednesday morning, on entering school, each pupil was expected to lay his exercise on Mr. Grimshaw's desk; the subject was usually selected by Mr. Grimshaw himself, the Monday previous. With a humor characteristic of him, our teacher had instituted two prizes, one for the best and the other for the worst composition of the month. The first prize consisted of a penknife, or a pencil-case, or some such article dear to the heart of youth; the second prize entitled the winner to wear for an hour or two a sort of conical paper cap, on the front of which was written, in tall letters, this modest admission: I AM A DUNCE! The competitor who took prize No. 2 wasn't generally an object of envy.

My pulse beat high with pride and expectation that Wednesday morning, as I laid my essay, neatly folded, on the master's table. I firmly decline to say which prize I won.

It is no small-author vanity that induces me to publish this stray leaf of natural history. I lay it before our young folks, not for their admiration, but for their criticism. Let each reader take his lead pencil and remorselessly correct the orthography, the capitalization, and the punctuation of the essay. I shall not feel a bit hurt at seeing my treatise cut all to pieces; though I think highly of the production, not on account of its literary excellence, which I candidly admit is not overpowering, but because it was written years and years ago about *Gypsy*, by a little fellow who, when I strive to recall him, appears to me like a reduced ghost of my present self; but here's the composition to speak for itself:

The Horse

*the horse is a usefull anemal He
is nice to have. i have one.
her name is gipsey. She bites, her
main is very long. one Day i was
washing her front Foot when she
bent down her head and lifted
me up by the trowser and tu
mbled me into the water Pale
that was standing near by. i hit*

her six times with a peace of hoop the way of the transgressor is hard

T. Bailey

I am confident that any reader who has ever had pets, birds or animals, will forgive me for this brief digression.

WINTER AT RIVERMOUTH

I GUESS we're going to have a regular old-fashioned snowstorm," said Captain Nutter, one bleak December morning, casting a peculiarly nautical glance skyward.

The Captain was always hazarding prophecies about the weather, which somehow never turned out according to his prognostications. The vanes on the church steeples seemed to take fiendish pleasure in humiliating the dear old gentleman. If he said it was going to be a clear day, a dense sea-fog was pretty certain to set in before noon. Once he caused a protracted drought by assuring us every morning, for six consecutive weeks, that it would rain in a few hours. But, sure enough, that afternoon it began snowing.

Now I had not seen a snowstorm since I was eighteen months old, and of course remembered nothing about it. A boy familiar from his infancy with the rigors of our New England winters can form no idea of the impression made on me by this natural phenomenon. My delight and surprise were as boundless as if the heavy gray sky had let down a shower of pond lilies and white roses, instead of snowflakes. It happened to be a half-holiday, so I had nothing to do but watch the feathery crystals whirling hither and thither through the air. I stood by the sitting-room window gazing at the wonder until twilight shut out the novel scene.

Several inches of snow had already fallen. The rose-bushes at the door drooped with the weight of their magical blossoms, and the two posts that held the garden gate were transformed into stately Turks, with white turbans, guarding the entrance to the Nutter House.

The storm increased at sundown, and continued with unabated violence through the night. The next morning, when I jumped out of bed, the sun was shining brightly, the cloudless heavens wore the tender azure of June, and the whole earth lay muffled up to the eyes, as it were, in a thick mantle of milk-white down.

It was a very deep snow. The Oldest Inhabitant (what would become of a New England town or village without its oldest inhabitant?) overhauled his almanacs, and pronounced it the deepest snow we had had for twenty years. It couldn't have been much deeper without smothering us all. Our street was a sight to be seen, or, rather, it was a sight not to be seen; for very little street was visible. One huge drift completely banked up our front door and half covered my bedroom window.

There was no school that day, for all the thoroughfares were impassable. By twelve o'clock, however, the great snow ploughs, each drawn by four yokes of oxen, broke a wagon path through the principal streets; but the foot passengers had a hard time of it floundering in the arctic drifts.

The Captain and I cut a tunnel, three feet wide and six feet high, from our front door to the sidewalk opposite. It was a beautiful cavern, with its walls and roof inlaid with mother-of-pearl and diamonds. I am sure the ice palace of the Russian Empress, in Cowper's poem, was not a more superb piece of architecture.

The thermometer began falling shortly before sunset, and we had the bitterest cold night I ever experienced. This brought out the Oldest Inhabitant again the next day—and what a gay old boy he was for deciding everything! Our tunnel was turned into solid ice. A crust thick enough to bear men and horses had formed over the snow everywhere, and the air was alive with merry sleighbells. Icy stalactites, a yard long, hung from the eaves of the houses, and the Turkish sentinels at the gate looked as if they intended never to be relieved from duty.

So the winter set in cold and glittering. Everything out of doors was sheathed in silver mail. To quote from Charley Marden, it was "cold enough to freeze the tail off a brass monkey"—an observation which seemed to me extremely happy, though I knew little or nothing concerning the endurance of brass monkeys, having never seen one.

I had looked forward to the advent of the season with grave apprehensions, nerving myself to meet dreary nights and monotonous days; but summer itself was not

more jolly than winter at Rivermouth. Snowballing at
school, skating on the Mill Dam, coasting by moonlight,
long rides behind Gypsy in a brand-new little sleigh built
expressly for her, were sports no less exhilarating than
those which belonged to the sunny months. And then
Thanksgiving! The nose of Memory—why shouldn't
Memory have a nose?—dilates with pleasure over the rich
perfume of Miss Abigail's forty mince pies, each one more
delightful than the other, like the Sultan's forty wives.
Christmas was another red-letter day, though it was not
so generally observed in New England as it is now.

The great wood fire in the tiled chimney place made our
sitting-room very cheerful of winter nights. When the
north wind howled about the eaves, and the sharp sleet
rattled against the windowpanes, it was nice to be so
warmly sheltered from the storm. A dish of apples and a
pitcher of chilly cider were always served during the evening. The Captain had a funny way of leaning back in
the chair, and eating his apple with his eyes closed. Sometimes I played dominos with him, and sometimes Miss
Abigail read aloud to us, pronouncing "to" *toe*, and
sounding all the *eds*.

In a former chapter I alluded to Miss Abigail's managing propensities. She had effected many changes in
the Nutter House before I came there to live; but there
was one thing against which
she had long contended without
being able to overcome it. This
was the Captain's pipe. On first
taking command of the household, she prohibited smoking in
the sitting-room, where it had

been the old gentleman's custom to take a whiff or two of
the fragrant weed after meals. The edict went forth—and
so did the pipe. An excellent move, no doubt; but then the
house was his, and if he saw fit to keep a tub of tobacco
burning in the middle of the parlor floor, he had a perfect
right to do so. However, he humored her in this as in other
matters, and smoked by stealth, like a guilty creature, in
the barn, or about the gardens. That was practicable in
summer, but in winter the Captain was hard put to it.
When he couldn't stand it longer, he retreated to his bedroom and barricaded the door. Such was the position of
affairs at the time of which I write.

One morning, a few days after the great snow, as Miss
Abigail was dusting the chronometer in the hall, she beheld Captain Nutter slowly descending the staircase, with
a long clay pipe in his mouth. Miss Abigail could hardly
credit her own eyes.

"Dan'el!" she gasped, retiring heavily on the hat rack.

The tone of reproach with which this word was uttered
failed to produce the slightest effect on the Captain, who
merely removed the pipe from his lips for an instant, and
blew a cloud into the chilly air. The thermometer stood at
two degrees below zero in our hall.

"Dan'el!" cried Miss Abigail, hysterically—"Dan'el,
don't come near me!" Whereupon she fainted away; for
the smell of tobacco smoke always made her deadly sick.

Kitty Collins rushed from the kitchen with a basin of
water, and set to work bathing Miss Abigail's temples and
chafing her hands. I thought my grandfather rather cruel,
as he stood there with a half-smile on his countenance,
complacently watching Miss Abigail's sufferings. When
she was "brought to," the Captain sat down beside her,

and, with a lovely twinkle in his eye, said softly: "Abigail, my dear, *there wasn't any tobacco in that pipe!* It was a new pipe. I fetched it down for Tom to blow soap bubbles with."

At these words Kitty Collins hurried away, her features working strangely. Several minutes later I came upon her in the scullery with the greater portion of a crash towel stuffed into her mouth. "Miss Abygil smelt the terbacca with her oi!" cried Kitty, partially removing the cloth, and then immediately stopping herself up again.

The Captain's joke furnished us— that is, Kitty and me—with mirth for many a day; as to Miss Abigail, I think she never wholly pardoned him. After this, Captain Nutter gradually gave up smoking, which is an untidy, injurious, disgraceful, and highly pleasant habit.

A boy's life in a secluded New England town in winter does not afford many points for illustration. Of course he gets his ears or toes frostbitten; of course he smashes his sled against another boy's; of course he bangs his head on the ice; and he's a lad of no enterprise whatever, if he doesn't manage to skate into an eel hole, and be brought home half drowned. All these things happened to me; but, as they lack novelty, I pass them over, to tell you about the famous snow fort which we built on Slatter's Hill.

THE SNOW FORT ON SLATTER'S HILL

THE memory of man, even that of the Oldest Inhabitant, runneth not back to the time when there did not exist a feud between the North End and the South End boys of Rivermouth.

The origin of the feud is involved in mystery; it is impossible to say which party was the first aggressor in the far-off ante-revolutionary ages; but the fact remains that the youngsters of those antipodal sections entertained a mortal hatred for each other, and that this hatred had been handed down from generation to generation, like Miles Standish's punchbowl.

118

I know not what laws, natural or unnatural, regulated the warmth of the quarrel; but at some seasons it raged more violently than at others. This winter, both parties were unusually lively and antagonistic. Great was the wrath of the South Enders, when they discovered that the North Enders had thrown up a fort on the crown of Slatter's Hill.

Slatter's Hill, or No-man's-land, as it was generally called, was a rise of ground covering, perhaps, an acre and a quarter, situated on an imaginary line, marking the boundary between the two districts. An immense stratum of granite, which here and there thrust out a wrinkled boulder, prevented the site from being used for building purposes. The street ran on either side of the hill, from one part of which a quantity of rock had been removed to form the underpinning of the new jail. This excavation made the approach from that point all but impossible, especially when the ragged ledges were a-glitter with ice. You see what a spot it was for a snow fort.

One evening twenty or thirty of the North Enders quietly took possession of Slatter's Hill, and threw up a strong line of breastworks, something after this shape:

The rear of the intrenchment, being protected by the quarry, was left open. The walls were four feet high, and twenty-two inches thick, strengthened at the angles by stakes driven firmly into the ground.

Fancy the rage of the South Enders the next day, when

they spied our snowy citadel, with Jack Harris's red silk pocket handkerchief floating defiantly from the flagstaff!

In less than an hour it was known all over town, in military circles at least, that the "Puddle-dockers" and the "River-rats" (these were the derisive sub-titles bestowed on our South End foes) intended to attack the fort that Saturday afternoon.

At two o'clock all the fighting boys of the Temple Grammar School, and as many recruits as we could muster, lay behind the walls of Fort Slatter, with three hundred compact snowballs piled up in pyramids, awaiting the approach of the enemy. The enemy was not slow in making his approach—fifty strong, headed by one Mat Ames. Our forces were under the command of General J. Harris.

Before the action commenced, a meeting was arranged between the rival commanders, who drew up and signed certain rules and regulations respecting the conduct of the battle. As it was impossible for the North Enders to occupy the fort permanently, it was stipulated that the South Enders should assault it only on Wednesday and Saturday afternoons between the hours of two and six. For them to take possession of the place at any other time was not to constitute a capture, but on the contrary was to be considered a dishonorable and cowardly act. The North Enders, on the other hand, agreed to give up the fort whenever ten of the storming party succeeded in obtaining at one time a footing on the parapet, and were able to hold the same for the space of two minutes. Both sides were to abstain from putting pebbles into their snow balls, nor was it permissible to use frozen ammunition. A snowball soaked in water and left out to cool was a projectile which in previous years had been resorted to with disastrous results.

These preliminaries settled, the commanders retired to their respective corps. The interview had taken place on the hillside between the opposing lines.

General Harris divided his men into two bodies: the first comprised the most skillful marksmen, or gunners; the second, the reserve force, was composed of the strongest boys, whose duty it was to repel the scaling parties, and to make occasional sallies for the purpose of capturing prisoners, who were bound by the articles of treaty to faithfully serve under our flag until they were exchanged at the close of the day.

The repellers were called light infantry; but when they carried on operations beyond the fort they became cavalry. It was also their duty, when not otherwise engaged, to manufacture snowballs. The General's staff consisted of five Templars (I among the number, with the rank of Major), who carried the General's orders and looked after the wounded.

General Mat Ames, a veteran commander, was no less wide awake in the disposition of his army. Five companies, each numbering but six men, in order not to present too big a target to our sharpshooters, were to charge the fort from different points, their advance being covered by a heavy fire from the gunners posted in the rear. Each scaler was provided with only two rounds of ammunition, which were not to be used until he had mounted the breastwork and could deliver his shots on our heads.

The following cut represents the interior of the fort just previous to the assault. Nothing on earth could represent the state of things after the first volley.

F. Flagstaff.
b. General Harris and his Staff.
c. Ammunition.
d. Hospital.

e e. Reserve corps.
f f. Gunners in position.
g g. The quarry.

The enemy was posted thus:

a a. The five attacking columns.   b b. Artillery.
c. General Ames's headquarters.

The thrilling moment had now arrived. If I had been going into a real engagement I could not have been more deeply impressed by the solemnity of the occasion.

The fort opened fire first—a single ball from the dexterous hand of General Harris taking General Ames in the very pit of his stomach. A cheer went up from Fort Slatter. In an instant the air was thick with flying missiles, in the midst of which we dimly descried the storming parties sweeping up the hill, shoulder to shoulder. The shouts of the leaders, and the snowballs bursting like shells about our ears, made it very lively.

Not more than a dozen of the enemy succeeded in reaching the crest of the hill; five of these clambered upon the icy walls, where they were instantly grabbed by the legs and jerked into the fort. The rest retired confused and blinded by our well-directed fire.

When General Harris (with his right eye bunged up) said, "Soldiers, I am proud of you!" my heart swelled in my bosom.

The victory, however, had not been without its price. Six North Enders, having rushed out to harass the discomfited enemy, were gallantly cut off by General Ames and captured. Among these were Lieutenant P. Whitcomb (who had no business to join in the charge, being weak in the knees), and Captain Fred Langdon, of General Harris's staff. Whitcomb was one of the most notable shots on our side, though he was not much to boast of in a rough-and-tumble fight, owing to the weakness before mentioned. General Ames put him among the gunners, and we were quickly made aware of the loss we had sustained, by receiving a frequent artful ball which seemed to light with unerring instinct on any nose that was the least bit exposed. I have known one of Pepper's snowballs, fired point-blank, to turn a corner and hit a boy who considered himself absolutely safe.

But we had no time for vain regrets. The battle raged. Already there were two bad cases of black eye, and one of nosebleed, in the hospital.

It was glorious excitement, those pell-mell onslaughts and hand-to-hand struggles. Twice we were within an ace of being driven from our stronghold, when General Harris and his staff leaped recklessly upon the ramparts and hurled the besiegers heels over head down hill.

At sunset, the garrison of Fort Slatter was still unconquered, and the South Enders, in a solid phalanx, marched off whistling "Yankee Doodle," while we cheered and jeered them until they were out of hearing.

General Ames remained behind to effect an exchange of prisoners. We held thirteen of his men, and he eleven of ours. General Ames proposed to call it an even thing, since many of his eleven prisoners were officers, while nearly all our thirteen captives were privates. A dispute arising on this point, the two noble generals came to fisticuffs, and in the fracas our brave commander got his remaining well eye badly damaged. This didn't prevent him from writing a general order the next day, on a slate, in which he complimented the troops on their heroic behavior.

On the following Wednesday the siege was renewed. I forget whether it was on that afternoon or the next that we lost Fort Slatter; but lose it we did, with much valuable ammunition and several men. After a series of desperate assaults, we forced General Ames to capitulate; and he, in turn, made the place too hot to hold us. So from day to day the tide of battle surged to and fro, sometimes favoring our arms, and sometimes those of the enemy.

General Ames handled his men with great skill; his deadliest foe could not deny that. Once he outgeneraled our commander in the following manner: he massed his gunners on our left and opened a brisk fire, under cover of which a single company (six men) advanced on that angle of the fort. Our reserves on the right rushed over to defend the threatened point. Meanwhile, four companies of the enemy's scalers made a detour round the foot of the hill, and dashed into Fort Slatter without opposition. At the same moment General Ames's gunners closed in on our left, and there we were between two fires. Of course we had to vacate the fort. A cloud rested on General Harris's military reputation until his superior tactics enabled him to dispossess the enemy.

As the winter wore on, the war spirit waxed fiercer and fiercer. At length the provision against using heavy sub-

stances in the snowballs was disregarded. A ball stuck full of sand-bird shot came tearing into Fort Slatter. In retaliation, General Harris ordered a broadside of shells; i. e. snowballs containing marbles. After this, both sides never failed to freeze their ammunition.

It was no longer child's play to march up to the walls of Fort Slatter, nor was the position of the besieged less perilous. At every assault three or four boys on each side were disabled. It was not an infrequent occurrence for the combatants to hold up a flag of truce while they removed some insensible comrade.

Matters grew worse and worse. Seven North Enders had been seriously wounded, and a dozen South Enders were reported on the sick list. The selectmen of the town awoke to the fact of what was going on, and detailed a posse of police to prevent further disturbance. The boys at the foot of the hill, South Enders as it happened, finding themselves assailed in the rear and on the flank, turned round and attempted to beat off the watchmen. In this they were sustained by numerous volunteers from the fort, who looked upon the interference as tyrannical.

The watch were determined fellows, and charged the boys valiantly, driving them all into the fort, where we made common cause, fighting side by side like the best of friends. In vain the four guardians of the peace rushed up the hill, flourishing their clubs and calling upon us to surrender. They could not get within ten yards of the fort, our fire was so destructive. In one of the onsets a man named Mugridge, more valorous than his peers, threw himself upon the parapet, when he was seized by twenty pairs of hands, and dragged inside the breastwork, where fifteen boys sat down on him to keep him quiet.

Perceiving that it was impossible with their small number to dislodge us, the watch sent for reinforcements. Their call was responded to, not only by the whole constabulary force (eight men), but by a numerous body of citizens, who had become alarmed at the prospect of a riot. This formidable array brought us to our senses: we began to think that maybe discretion was the better part of valor. General Harris and General Ames, with their respective staffs, held a council of war in the hospital, and a backward movement was decided on. So, after one grand farewell volley, we fled, sliding, jumping, rolling, tumbling down the quarry at the rear of the fort, and escaped without losing a man.

But we lost Fort Slatter forever. Those battle-scarred ramparts were razed to the ground, and humiliating ashes sprinkled over the historic spot, near which a solitary lynx-eyed policeman was seen prowling from time to time during the rest of the winter.

The event passed into a legend, and afterwards, when later instances of pluck and endurance were spoken of, the boys would say, "By golly! you ought to have been at the fights on Slatter's Hill!"

FOURTEEN

THE CRUISE OF THE DOLPHIN

IT WAS spring again. The snow had faded away
like a dream, and we were awakened, so to speak, by
the sudden chirping of robins in our back garden. Mar-
velous transformation of snowdrifts into lilacs, wondrous
miracle of the unfolding leaf! We read in the Holy Book
how our Saviour, at the marriage feast, changed the water
into wine; we pause and wonder; but every hour a greater
miracle is wrought at our very feet, if we have but eyes
to see it.

I had now been a year at Rivermouth. If you do not
know what sort of a boy I was, it is not because I haven't
been frank with you. Of my progress at school I say little;
for this is a story, pure and simple, and not a treatise on
education. Behold me, however, well up in most of the
classes. I have worn my Latin grammar into tatters, and
am in the first book of Virgil. I interlard my conversation
at home with easy quotations from that poet, and impress
Captain Nutter with a lofty notion of my learning. I am

likewise translating *Les Aventures de Télémaque* from the French, and shall tackle Blair's *Lectures* the next term. I am ashamed of my crude composition about The Horse, and can do better now. Sometimes my head almost aches with the variety of my knowledge. I consider Mr. Grimshaw the greatest scholar that ever lived, and I don't know which I would rather be—a learned man like him, or a circus rider.

My thoughts revert to this particular spring more frequently than to any other period of my boyhood, for it was marked by an event that left an indelible impression on my memory. As I pen these pages, I feel that I am writing of something which happened yesterday, so vividly it all comes back to me.

Every Rivermouth boy looks upon the sea as being in some way mixed up with his destiny. While he is yet a baby lying in his cradle, he hears the dull, far-off boom of the breakers; when he is older, he wanders by the sandy shore, watching the waves that come plunging up the beach like white-maned sea-horses, as Thoreau calls them; his eye follows the lessening sail as it fades into the blue horizon, and he burns for the time when he shall stand on the quarterdeck of his own ship, and go sailing proudly across that mysterious waste of waters.

Then the town itself is full of hints and flavors of the sea. The gables and roofs of the houses facing eastward are covered with red rust, like the flukes of old anchors; a salty smell pervades the air, and dense gray fogs, the very breath of Ocean, periodically creep up into the quiet streets and envelop everything. The terrific storms that lash the coast; the kelp and spars, and sometimes the bodies of drowned men, tossed on shore by the scornful waves; the shipyards, the wharves, and the tawny fleet of fishing smacks yearly fitted out at Rivermouth—these things, and a hundred other, feed the imagination and fill the brain of every healthy boy with dreams of adventure. He learns to swim almost as soon as he can walk; he draws in with his mother's milk the art of handling an oar: he is born a sailor, whatever he may turn out to be afterwards.

To own the whole or a portion of a rowboat is his earliest ambition. No wonder that I, born to this life, and coming back to it with freshest sympathies, should have caught the prevailing infection. No wonder I longed to buy a part of the trim little sailboat *Dolphin*, which chanced just then to be in the market. This was in the latter part of May.

Three shares, at five or six dollars each, I forget which, had already been taken by Phil Adams, Fred Langdon, and Binny Wallace. The fourth and remaining share hung fire. Unless a purchaser could be found for this, the bargain was to fall through.

I am afraid I required but slight urging to join in the investment. I had four dollars and fifty cents on hand, and the treasurer of the Centipedes advanced me the balance, receiving my silver pencil-case as ample security. It was a proud moment when I stood on the wharf with my partners, inspecting the *Dolphin*, moored at the foot of a very slippery flight of steps. She was painted white with a green stripe outside, and on the stern a yellow dolphin, with its scarlet mouth wide open, stared with a surprised expression at its own reflection in the water. The boat was a great bargain.

I whirled my cap in the air, and ran to the stairs leading down from the wharf, when a hand was laid gently on my shoulder. I turned, and faced Captain Nutter. I never saw such an old sharp-eye as he was in those days.

I knew he wouldn't be angry with me for buying a row-boat; but I also knew that the little bowsprit suggesting a

jib, and the tapering mast ready for its few square yards of canvas, were trifles not likely to meet his approval. As far as rowing on the river, among the wharves, was concerned, the Captain had long since withdrawn his decided objections, having convinced himself, by going out with me several times, that I could manage a pair of sculls as well as anybody.

I was right in my surmises. He commanded me, in the most emphatic terms, never to go out in the *Dolphin* without leaving the mast in the boathouse. This curtailed my anticipated sport, but the pleasure of having a pull whenever I wanted it remained. I never disobeyed the Captain's orders touching the sail, though I sometimes extended my row beyond the points he had indicated.

The river was dangerous for sailboats. Squalls, without the slightest warning, were of frequent occurrence;

scarcely a year passed that six or seven persons were not drowned under the very windows of the town, and these, oddly enough, were generally sea captains, who either did not understand the river, or lacked the skill to handle a small craft.

A knowledge of such disasters, one of which I witnessed, consoled me somewhat when I saw Phil Adams skimming over the water in a spanking breeze with every stitch of canvas set. There were few better yachtsmen than Phil Adams. He usually went sailing alone, for both Fred Langdon and Binny Wallace were under the same restrictions I was.

Not long after the purchase of the boat, we planned an excursion to Sandpeep Island, the last of the islands in the harbor. We proposed to start early in the morning, and return with the tide in the moonlight. Our only difficulty was to obtain a whole day's exemption from school, the customary half-holiday not being long enough for our picnic. Somehow, we couldn't work it; but fortune arranged it for us. I may say here, that, whatever else I did, I never played truant ("hookey" we called it) in my life.

One afternoon the four owners of the *Dolphin* exchanged significant glances when Mr. Grimshaw announced from the desk that there would be no school the following day, he having just received intelligence of the death of his uncle in Boston. I was sincerely attached to Mr. Grimshaw, but I am afraid that the death of his uncle did not affect me as it ought to have done.

We were up before sunrise the next morning, in order to take advantage of the flood tide, which waits for no man. Our preparations for the cruise were made the previous evening. In the way of eatables and drinkables, we had stored in the stern of the *Dolphin* a generous bag of hardtack (for the chowder), a piece of pork to fry the cunners in, three gigantic apple pies (bought at Pettingil's), half a dozen lemons, and a keg of spring water —the last-named article we slung over the side, to keep it cool, as soon as we got under way. The crockery and the bricks for our camp stove we placed in the bows with the groceries, which included sugar, pepper, salt, and a bottle of pickles. Phil Adams contributed to the outfit a small tent of unbleached cotton cloth, under which we intended to take our nooning.

We unshipped the mast, threw in an extra oar, and were ready to embark. I do not believe that Christopher Columbus, when he started on his rather successful voyage of discovery, felt half the responsibility and importance that weighed upon me as I sat on the middle seat of the *Dolphin*, with my oar resting in the rowlock. I wonder if Christopher Columbus quietly slipped out of the house without letting his estimable family know what he was up to?

Charley Marden, whose father had promised to cane him if he ever stepped foot on sail or rowboat, came down to the wharf in a sour-grape humor, to see us off. Nothing would tempt *him* to go out on the river in such a crazy clamshell of a boat. He pretended that he did not expect to behold us alive again, and tried to throw a wet blanket over the expedition.

"Guess you'll have a squally time of it," said Charley, casting off the painter. "I'll drop in at old Newbury's" (Newbury was the parish undertaker) "and leave word, as I go along!"

"Bosh!" muttered Phil Adams, sticking the boat hook into the stringpiece of the wharf, and sending the *Dolphin* half a dozen yards towards the current.

How calm and lovely the river was! Not a ripple stirred on the glassy surface, broken only by the sharp cutwater of our tiny craft. The sun, as round and red as an August moon, was by this time peering above the waterline.

The town had drifted behind us, and we were entering among the group of islands. Sometimes we could almost touch with our boat hook the shelving banks on either side. As we neared the mouth of the harbor, a little breeze now and then wrinkled the blue water, shook the spangles from the foliage, and gently lifted the spiral mist-wreaths that still clung along shore. The measured dip of our oars and the drowsy twitterings of the birds seemed to mingle with, rather than break, the enchanted silence that reigned about us.

The scent of the new clover comes back to me now, as I recall that delicious morning when we floated away in a fairy boat down a river like a dream!

The sun was well up when the nose of the *Dolphin* nestled against the snow-white bosom of Sandpeep Island. This island, as I have said before, was the last of the cluster, one side of it being washed by the sea. We landed on the river side, the sloping sands and quiet water affording us a good place to moor the boat.

It took us an hour or two to transport our stores to the spot selected for the encampment. Having pitched our tent, using the five oars to support the canvas, we got out our lines, and went down the rocks seaward to fish. It was early for cunners, but we were lucky enough to catch as nice a mess as ever you saw. A cod for the chowder was not so easily secured. At last Binny Wallace hauled in a plump little fellow crusted all over with flaky silver.

To skin the fish, build our fireplace, and cook the dinner kept us busy the next two hours. The fresh air and the exercise had given us the appetites of wolves, and we were about famished by the time the savory mixture was ready for our clamshell saucers.

I shall not insult the rising generation on the seaboard by telling them how delectable is a chowder compounded and eaten in this Robinson Crusoe fashion. As for the boys who live inland, and know naught of such marine feasts, my heart is full of pity for them. What wasted lives! Not to know the delights of a clambake, not to love chowder, to be ignorant of lobscouse!

How happy we were, we four, sitting cross-legged in the crisp salt grass, with the invigorating sea breeze blowing gratefully through our hair! What a joyous thing was life, and how far off seemed death—death, that lurks in all pleasant places, and was so near!

The banquet finished, Phil Adams drew forth from his pocket a handful of sweet-fern cigars; but as none of the party could indulge without imminent risk of becoming sick, we all, on one pretext or another, declined, and Phil smoked by himself.

The wind had freshened by this, and we found it comfortable to put on the jackets which had been thrown aside in the heat of the day. We strolled along the beach and gathered large quantities of the fairy-woven Iceland moss, which, at certain seasons, is washed to these shores; then we played at ducks and drakes, and then, the sun being sufficiently low, we went in bathing.

Before our bath was ended a slight change had come over the sky and sea; fleecy white clouds scudded here and there, and a muffled moan from the breakers caught our ears from time to time. While we were dressing, a few hurried drops of rain came lisping down, and we adjourned to the tent to await the passing of the squall.

"We're all right, anyhow," said Phil Adams. "It won't be much of a blow, and we'll be as snug as a bug in a rug, here in the tent, particularly if we have that lemonade which some of you fellows were going to make."

By an oversight, the lemons had been left in the boat. Binny Wallace volunteered to go for them.

"Put an extra stone on the painter, Binny," said Adams, calling after him; "it would be awkward to have the *Dolphin* give us the slip and return to port minus her passengers."

"That it would," answered Binny, scrambling down the rocks.

Sandpeep Island is diamond-shaped—one point running out into the sea, and the other looking towards the town. Our tent was on the river side. Though the *Dolphin* was also on the same side, it lay out of sight by the beach at the farther extremity of the island.

Binny Wallace had been absent five or six minutes, when we heard him calling our several names in tones that indicated distress or surprise, we could not tell which. Our first thought was, "The boat has broken adrift!"

We sprang to our feet and hastened down to the beach. On turning the bluff which hid the mooring place from our view, we found the conjecture correct. Not only was the *Dolphin* afloat, but poor little Binny Wallace was standing in the bows with his arms stretched helplessly towards us—*drifting out to sea!*

"Head the boat in shore!" shouted Phil Adams.

Wallace ran to the tiller; but the slight cockle shell merely swung round and drifted broadside on. Oh, if we had but left a single scull in the *Dolphin!*

"Can you swim it?" cried Adams, desperately, using his

hand as a speaking-trumpet, for the distance between the boat and the island widened momently.

Binny Wallace looked down at the sea, which was covered with white caps, and made a despairing gesture. He knew, and we knew, that the stoutest swimmer could not live forty seconds in those angry waters.

A wild, insane light came into Phil Adams's eyes, as he stood knee deep in boiling surf, and for an instant I think he meditated plunging into the ocean after the receding boat.

The sky darkened, and an ugly look stole rapidly over the broken surface of the sea.

Binny Wallace half rose from his seat in the stern, and waved his hand to us in token of farewell. In spite of the distance, increasing every instant, we could see his face plainly. The anxious expression it wore at first had passed. It was pale and meek now, and I love to think there was a kind of halo about it, like that which painters place around the forehead of a saint. So he drifted away.

The sky grew darker and darker. It was only by straining our eyes through the unnatural twilight that we could keep the *Dolphin* in sight. The figure of Binny Wallace was no longer visible, for the boat itself had dwindled to a mere white dot on the black water. Now we lost it, and our hearts stopped throbbing; and now the speck appeared again, for an instant, on the crest of a high wave.

Finally, it went out like a spark, and we saw it no more. Then we gazed at each other, and dared not speak.

Absorbed in following the course of the boat, we had scarcely noticed the huddled inky clouds that sagged down all around us. From these threatening masses, seamed at intervals with pale lightning, there now burst a heavy peal of thunder that shook the ground under our feet. A sudden squall struck the sea, ploughing deep white furrows into it, and at the same instant a single piercing shriek rose above the tempest—the frightened cry of a gull swooping over the island. How it startled us!

It was impossible to keep our footing on the beach any longer. The wind and the breakers would have swept us into the ocean if we had not clung to each other with the desperation of drowning men. Taking advantage of a momentary lull, we crawled up the sands on our hands and knees, and, pausing in the lee of the granite ledge to gain breath, returned to the camp, where we found that the gale had snapped all the fastenings of the tent but one. Held by this, the puffed-out canvas swayed in the wind like a balloon. It was a task of some difficulty to secure it, which we did by beating down the canvas with the oars.

After several trials, we succeeded in setting up the tent on the leeward side of the ledge. Blinded by the vivid flashes of lightning, and drenched by the rain, which fell in torrents, we crept, half dead with fear and anguish, under our flimsy shelter. Neither the anguish nor the fear was on our own account, for we were comparatively safe, but for poor little Binny Wallace, driven out to sea in the merciless gale. We shuddered to think of him in that frail shell, drifting on and on to his grave, the sky rent with lightning over his head, and the green abysses yawning beneath him. We fell to crying, the three of us, and cried I know not how long.

Meanwhile the storm raged with augmented fury. We were obliged to hold on to the ropes of the tent to prevent it blowing away. The spray from the river leaped several

yards up the rocks and clutched at us malignantly. The
very island trembled with the concussions of the sea beating upon it, and at times I fancied that it had broken loose
from its foundation, and was floating off with us. The
breakers, streaked with angry phosphorus, were fearful to
look at.

The wind rose higher and higher, cutting long slits in
the tent, through which the rain poured incessantly. To
complete the sum of our miseries, the night was at hand.
It came down suddenly, at last, like a curtain, shutting in
Sandpeep Island from all the world.

It was a dirty night, as the sailors say. The darkness
was something that could be felt as well as seen—it
pressed down upon one with a cold, clammy touch. Gazing
into the hollow blackness, all sorts of imaginable shapes
seemed to start forth from vacancy—brilliant colors,
stars, prisms, and dancing lights. What boy, lying awake
at night, has not amused or terrified himself by peopling
the spaces round his bed with these phenomena of his own
eyes?

"I say," whispered Fred Langdon, at length, clutching
my hand, "don't you see things—out there—in the dark?"

"Yes, yes—Binny Wallace's face!"

I added to my own nervousness by making this avowal;
though for the last ten minutes I had seen little besides
that star-pale face with its angelic hair and brows. First
a slim yellow circle, like the nimbus round the moon, took
shape and grew sharp against the darkness; then this
faded gradually, and there was the Face, wearing the
same sad, sweet look it wore when he waved his hand to us
across the awful water. This optical illusion kept repeat-
ing itself.

"And I, too," said Adams. "I see it every now and then, outside there. What wouldn't I give if it really was poor little Wallace looking in at us! Oh boys, how shall we dare to go back to the town without him? I've wished a hundred times, since we've been sitting here, that I was in his place, alive or dead!"

We dreaded the approach of morning as much as we longed for it. The morning would tell us all. Was it possible for the *Dolphin* to outride such a storm? There was a lighthouse on Mackerel Reef, which lay directly in the course the boat had taken, when it disappeared. If the *Dolphin* had caught on this reef, perhaps Binny Wallace was safe. Perhaps his cries had been heard by the keeper of the light. The man owned a lifeboat, and had rescued several people. Who could tell?

Such were the questions we asked ourselves again and again, as we lay in each other's arms waiting for daybreak. What an endless night it was! I have known months that did not seem so long.

Our position was irksome rather than perilous; for the day was certain to bring us relief from the town, where our prolonged absence, together with the storm, had no doubt excited the liveliest alarm for our safety. But the cold, the darkness, and the suspense were hard to bear.

Our soaked jackets had chilled us to the bone. To keep warm, we lay huddled together so closely that we could hear our hearts beat above the tumult of sea and sky.

We used to laugh at Fred Langdon for always carrying in his pocket a small vial of essence of peppermint or sassafras, a few drops of which, sprinkled on a lump of loaf sugar, he seemed to consider a great luxury. I don't know what would have become of us at this crisis, if it hadn't been for that omnipresent bottle of hot stuff. We poured the stinging liquid over our sugar, which had kept dry in a sardine box, and warmed ourselves with frequent doses.

After four or five hours the rain ceased, the wind died away to a moan, and the sea—no longer raging like a maniac—sobbed and sobbed with a piteous human voice all along the coast. And well it might, after that night's work. Twelve sail of the Gloucester fishing fleet had gone down with every soul on board, just outside of Whale's Back light. Think of the wide grief that follows in the wake of one wreck; then think of the despairing women who wrung their hands and wept, the next morning, in the streets of Gloucester, Marblehead, and Newcastle!

Though our strength was nearly spent, we were too cold to sleep. Once I sunk into a troubled doze, when I seemed to hear Charley Marden's parting words, only it was the Sea that said them. After that I threw off the drowsiness whenever it threatened to overcome me.

Fred Langdon was the earliest to discover a filmy, luminous streak in the sky, the first glimmering of sunrise.

"Look, it is nearly daybreak!"

While we were following the direction of his finger, a sound of distant oars fell on our ears.

We listened breathlessly, and as the dip of the blades became more audible, we discerned two foggy lights, like will-o'-the-wisps, floating on the river.

Running down to the water's edge, we hailed the boats with all our might. The call was heard, for the oars rested a moment in the rowlocks, and then pulled in towards the island.

It was two boats from the town, in the foremost of which we could now make out the figures of Captain Nutter and Binny Wallace's father. We shrunk back on seeing *him*.

"Thank God!" cried Mr. Wallace, fervently, as he leaped from the wherry without waiting for the bow to touch the beach.

But when he saw only three boys standing on the sands, his eye wandered restlessly about in quest of the fourth; then a deadly pallor overspread his features.

Our story was soon told. A solemn silence fell upon the crowd of rough boatmen gathered round, interrupted only by a stifled sob from one poor old man, who stood apart from the rest.

The sea was still running too high for any small boat to venture out; so it was arranged that the wherry should take us back to town, leaving the yawl, with a picked crew, to hug the island until daybreak, and then set forth in search of the *Dolphin*.

Though it was barely sunrise when we reached town, there were a great many people assembled at the landing, eager for intelligence from missing boats. Two picnic parties had started downriver the day before, just previous to the gale, and nothing had been heard of them. It turned out that the pleasure-seekers saw their danger in time, and ran ashore on one of the least exposed islands, where they passed the night. Shortly after our own arrival they appeared off Rivermouth, much to the joy of their friends, in two shattered, dismasted boats.

The excitement over, I was in a forlorn state, physically and mentally. Captain Nutter put me to bed between hot blankets, and sent Kitty Collins for the doctor. I was wandering in my mind, and fancied myself still on Sandpeep

Island: now I gave orders to Wallace how to manage the boat, and now I cried because the rain was pouring in on me through the holes in the tent. Towards evening a high fever set in, and it was many days before my grandfather deemed it prudent to tell me that the *Dolphin* had been found, floating keel upwards, four miles southeast of Mackerel Reef.

Poor little Binny Wallace! How strange it seemed, when I went to school again, to see that empty seat in the fifth row! How gloomy the playground was, lacking the sunshine of his gentle, sensitive face! One day a folded sheet slipped from my algebra; it was the last note he ever wrote me. I couldn't read it for the tears.

What a pang shot across my heart the afternoon it was whispered through the town that a body had been washed ashore at Grave Point—the place where we bathed. We bathed there no more! How well I remember the funeral, and what a piteous sight it was afterwards to see his familiar name on a small headstone in the Old South Burying Ground!

Poor little Binny Wallace! Always the same to me. The rest of us have grown up into hard, worldly men, fighting the fight of life; but you are forever young, and gentle, and pure; a part of my own childhood that time cannot wither; always a little boy, always poor little Binny Wallace!

AN OLD ACQUAINTANCE TURNS UP

A YEAR had stolen by since the death of Binny Wallace—a year of which I have nothing important to record.

The loss of our little playmate threw a shadow over our young lives for many and many a month. The *Dolphin* rose and fell with the tide at the foot of the slippery steps, unused, the rest of the summer. At the close of November we hauled her sadly into the boathouse for the winter; but when spring came round we launched the *Dolphin* again, and often went down to the wharf and looked at her lying in the tangled eel grass, without much inclination to take a row. The associations connected with the boat were too painful as yet; but time, which wears the sharp edge from everything, softened this feeling, and one afternoon we brought out the cobwebbed oars.

The ice once broken, brief trips along the wharves— we seldom cared to go out into the river now—became one of our chief amusements. Meanwhile Gypsy was not forgotten. Every clear morning I was in the saddle before breakfast, and there are few roads or lanes within ten miles of Rivermouth that have not borne the print of her vagrant hoof.

I studied like a good fellow this quarter, carrying off a

couple of first prizes. The Captain expressed his gratification by presenting me with a new silver dollar. If a dollar in his eyes was smaller than a cartwheel, it wasn't so very much smaller. I redeemed my pencil-case from the treasurer of the Centipedes, and felt that I was getting on in the world.

It was at this time I was greatly cast down by a letter from my father saying that he should be unable to visit Rivermouth until the following year. With that letter came another to Captain Nutter, which he did not read aloud to the family, as usual. It was on business, he said, folding it up in his wallet. He received several of these business letters from time to time, and I noticed that they always made him silent and moody.

The fact is, my father's banking house was not thriving. The unlooked-for failure of a firm largely indebted to him had crippled "the house." When the Captain imparted this information to me, I didn't trouble myself over the matter. I supposed—if I supposed anything—that all grown-up people had more or less money, when they wanted it. Whether they inherited it, or whether the government supplied them, was not clear to me. A loose idea that my father had a private gold mine somewhere or other relieved me of all uneasiness.

I was not far from right. Every man has within himself a gold mine whose riches are limited only by his own industry. It is true, it sometimes happens that industry does not avail, if a man lacks that something which, for want of a better name, we call Luck. My father was a person of untiring energy and ability; but he had no luck. To use a Rivermouth saying, he was always catching sculpins when everyone else with the same bait was catching mackerel.

It was more than two years since I had seen my parents. I felt that I could not bear a longer separation. Every letter from New Orleans—we got two or three a month— gave me a fit of homesickness; and when it was definitely settled that my father and mother were to remain in the South another twelvemonth, I resolved to go to them.

Since Binny Wallace's death, Pepper Whitcomb had been my *fidus Achates;* we occupied desks near each other at school, and were always together in play hours. We shared our pocket money and our secrets—those amazing secrets which boys have. We met in lonely places by stealth, and parted like conspirators; we couldn't buy a jackknife or build a kite without throwing an air of mystery and guilt over the transaction.

I naturally hastened to lay my New Orleans project before Pepper Whitcomb, having dragged him for that purpose to a secluded spot in the dark pine woods outside the town. Pepper listened to me with a gravity which he will not be able to surpass when he becomes Chief Justice, and strongly advised me to go.

"The summer vacation," said Pepper, "lasts six weeks; that will give you a fortnight to spend in New Orleans, allowing two weeks each way for the journey."

I wrung his hand and begged him to accompany me, offering to defray all the expenses. I wasn't anything if I wasn't princely, in those days. After considerable urging, he consented to go on terms so liberal. The whole thing was arranged; there was nothing to do now but to advise Captain Nutter of my plan.

The possibility that he might oppose the tour never entered my head. I was therefore totally unprepared for the vigorous negative which met my proposal. I was deeply mortified, moreover, for there was Pepper Whitcomb on the wharf, at the foot of the street, waiting for me to come and let him know what day we were to start.

"Go to New Orleans? Go to Jericho!" exclaimed Captain Nutter. "You'd look pretty, you two, philandering off, like the babes in the wood, twenty-five hundred miles, 'with all the world before you where to choose'!"

And the Captain's features, which had worn an indignant air as he began the sentence, relaxed into a broad smile. Whether it was at the felicity of his own quotation, or at the mental picture he drew of Pepper and myself on our travels, I couldn't tell, and I didn't care. I was heartbroken. I felt a trifle sheepish, too, about facing my chum after all the dazzling inducements I had held out to him.

My grandfather, seeing that I took the matter seriously, pointed out the difficulties of such a journey and the great expense involved. He entered into the details of my father's money troubles, and succeeded in making it plain to me that my wishes, under the circumstances, were somewhat unreasonable. It was in no cheerful mood that I joined Pepper at the end of the wharf.

I found that young gentleman leaning against the bulkhead gazing intently towards the islands in the harbor. He had formed a telescope of his hands, and was so occupied with his observations as to be oblivious of my approach.

"Hullo!" cried Pepper, dropping his hands. "Look there! isn't that a bark coming up the Narrows?"

"Where?"

"Just at the left of Fishcrate Island. Don't you see the foremast peeping above the old derrick?"

Sure enough it was a vessel of considerable size, slowly

beating up to town. In a few moments more the other two masts were visible above the green hillocks.

"Fore-topmasts blown away," said Pepper. "Putting in for repairs, I guess."

As the bark lazily crept from behind the last of the islands, she let go her anchors and swung round with the tide. Then the gleeful chant of the sailors at the capstan came to us pleasantly across the water. The vessel lay within three-quarters of a mile of us, and we could plainly see the men at the davits lowering the starboard longboat. It no sooner touched the stream than a dozen of the crew scrambled like mice over the side of the merchantman.

In a neglected seaport like Rivermouth the arrival of a large ship is an event of moment. The prospect of having twenty or thirty jolly tars let loose on the peaceful town excites divers emotions among the inhabitants. The small shopkeepers along the wharves anticipate a thriving trade: the proprietors of the two rival boarding-houses—the "Wee Drop" and the "Mariner's Home"—hasten down to the landing to secure lodgers; and the female population of Anchor Lane turn out to a woman, for a ship fresh from sea is always full of possible husbands and long-lost prodigal sons.

But, aside from this, there is scant welcome given to a ship's crew in Rivermouth. The toil-worn mariner is a sad fellow ashore, judging him by a severe moral standard.

Once, I remember, a United States frigate came into port for repairs after a storm. She lay in the river a fortnight or more, and every day sent us a gang of sixty or seventy of our country's gallant defenders, who spread themselves over the town, doing all sorts of mad things.

They were good-natured enough, but full of old Sancho. The "Wee Drop" proved a drop too much for many of them. They went singing through the streets at midnight, wringing off door knockers, shinning up water spouts, and frightening the Oldest Inhabitant nearly to death by popping their heads into his second-story window, and shouting "Fire!" One morning a blue-jacket was discovered in a perilous plight, halfway up the steeple of the South Church, clinging to the lightning rod. How he got there nobody could tell, not even blue-jacket himself. All he knew was, that the leg of his trousers had caught on a nail, and there he stuck, unable to move either way. It cost the town twenty dollars to get him down again. He directed the workmen how to splice the ladders brought to his assistance, and called his rescuers "butter-fingered landlubbers" with delicious coolness.

But those were man-of-war's men. The sedate-looking craft now lying off Fishcrate Island wasn't likely to carry any such cargo. Nevertheless we watched the coming in of the longboat with considerable interest.

As it drew near, the figure of the man pulling the stroke oar seemed oddly familiar to me. Where could I have seen him before? When and where? His back was towards me, but there was something about that closely cropped head that I recognized instantly.

"Way enough!" cried the steersman, and all the oars stood upright in the air. The man in the bow seized the boat hook, and, turning round quickly, showed me the honest face of Sailor Ben of the *Typhoon*.

"It's Sailor Ben!" I cried, nearly pushing Pepper Whitcomb overboard in my excitement.

Sailor Ben, with the wonderful pink lady on his arm, and the ships and stars and anchors tattooed all over him, was a well-known hero among my playmates. And there he was, like something in a dream come true!

I didn't wait for my old acquaintance to get firmly on the wharf, before I grasped his hand in both of mine.

"Sailor Ben, don't you remember me?"

He evidently did not. He shifted his quid from one cheek to the other, and looked at me meditatively.

"Lord luv ye, lad, I don't know you. I was never here afore in my life."

"What!" I cried, enjoying his perplexity, "have you forgotten the voyage from New Orleans in the *Typhoon*, two years ago, you lovely old picturebook?"

Ah! then he knew me, and in token of the recollection

gave my hand such a squeeze that I am sure an unpleasant change came over my countenance.

"Bless my eyes, but you have growed so! I shouldn't have knowed you if I had met you in Singapore!"

Without stopping to inquire, as I was tempted to do, why he was more likely to recognize me in Singapore than anywhere else, I invited him to come at once up to the Nutter House, where I insured him a warm welcome from the Captain.

"Hold steady, Master Tom," said Sailor Ben, slipping the painter through the ringbolt and tying the loveliest knot you ever saw; "hold steady till I see if the mate can let me off. If you please, sir," he continued, addressing the steersman, a very red-faced, bowlegged person, "this here is a little shipmate o' mine as wants to talk over back times along of me, if so it's convenient."

"All right, Ben," returned the mate, "sha'n't want you for an hour."

Leaving one man in charge of the boat, the mate and the rest of the crew went off together. In the meanwhile Pepper Whitcomb had got out his cunner-line, and was quietly fishing at the end of the wharf, as if to give me the idea that he wasn't so very much impressed by my intimacy with so renowned a character as Sailor Ben. Perhaps Pepper was a little jealous. At any rate, he refused to go with us to the house.

Captain Nutter was at home reading the *Rivermouth Barnacle*. He was a reader to do an editor's heart good; he never skipped over an advertisement, even if he had read it fifty times before. Then the paper went the rounds of the neighborhood, among the poor people, like the single portable eye which the three blind crones passed

to each other in the legend of King Acrisius. The Captain,
I repeat, was wandering in the labyrinths of the *Rivermouth Barnacle* when I led Sailor Ben into the sitting-
room.

My grandfather, whose inborn courtesy knew no dis-
tinctions, received my nautical friend as if he had been an
admiral instead of a common forecastle hand. Sailor Ben
pulled an imaginary tuft of hair on his forehead, and
bowed clumsily. Sailors have a way of using their forelock
as a sort of handle to bow with.

The old tar had probably never been in so handsome an
apartment in all his days, and nothing could induce him
to take the inviting mahogany chair which the Captain
wheeled out from the corner.

The abashed mariner stood up against the wall, twirling his tarpaulin in his two hands and looking extremely silly. He made a poor show in a gentleman's drawing-room, but what a fellow he had been in his day, when the gale blew great guns and the topsails wanted reefing! I thought of him with the Mexican squadron off Vera Cruz, where

The ringing battle-bolt sung from the three-decker out of
the foam,

and he didn't seem awkward or ignoble to me, for all his shyness.

As Sailor Ben declined to sit down, the Captain did not resume his seat; so we three stood in a constrained manner until my grandfather went to the door and called to Kitty to bring in a decanter of Madeira and two glasses.

"My grandson, here, has talked so much about you," said the Captain, pleasantly, "that you seem quite like an old acquaintance to me."

"Thankee, sir, thankee," returned Sailor Ben, looking as guilty as if he had been detected in picking a pocket.

"And I'm very glad to see you, Mr.—Mr.—"

"Sailor Ben," suggested that worthy.

"Mr. Sailor Ben," added the Captain, smiling. "Tom, open the door, there's Kitty with the glasses."

I opened the door, and Kitty entered the room bringing the things on a waiter, which she was about to set on the table, when suddenly she uttered a loud shriek; the decanter and glasses fell with a crash to the floor, and Kitty, as white as a sheet, was seen flying through the hall.

"It's his wraith! It's his wraith *!" we heard Kitty shrieking, in the kitchen.

* Ghost, spirit.

My grandfather and I turned with amazement to Sailor Ben. His eyes were standing out of his head like a lobster's.

"It's my own little Irish lass!" shouted the sailor, and he darted into the hall after her.

Even then we scarcely caught the meaning of his words, but when we saw Sailor Ben and Kitty sobbing on each other's shoulder in the kitchen, we understood it all.

"I begs your honor's parden, sir," said Sailor Ben, lifting his tear-stained face above Kitty's tumbled hair; "I begs your honor's parden for kicking up a rumpus in the house, but it's my own little Irish lass as I lost so long ago!"

"Heaven preserve us!" cried the Captain, blowing his nose violently—a transparent dodge to hide his emotion.

Miss Abigail was in an upper chamber, sweeping; but on hearing the unusual racket below, she scented an accident and came ambling downstairs with a bottle of the infallible hot drops in her hand. Nothing but the firmness of my grandfather prevented her from giving Sailor Ben a tablespoonful on the spot. But when she learned what had come about—that this was Kitty's husband, that Kitty Collins wasn't Kitty Collins now, but Mrs. Benjamin Watson, of Nantucket—the good soul sat down on the meal chest and sobbed as if—to quote from Captain Nutter—as if a husband of her own had turned up!

A happier set of people than we were never met together in a dingy kitchen or anywhere else. The Captain ordered a fresh decanter of Madeira, and made all hands, excepting myself, drink a cup to the return of "the prodigal sea-son," as he persisted in calling Sailor Ben.

When Sailor Ben's hour had expired, we walked with him down to the wharf, where the Captain held a consultation with the mate, which resulted in an extension of Mr. Watson's leave of absence, and afterwards in his discharge from his ship. We then went to the "Mariner's Home" to engage a room for him, as he wouldn't hear of accepting the hospitalities of the Nutter House.

"You see, I'm only an uneddicated man," he remarked to my grandfather, by way of explanation.

IN WHICH SAILOR BEN
SPINS A YARN

OF COURSE we were all very curious to learn what had befallen Sailor Ben that morning long ago, when he bade his little bride good-by, and disappeared so mysteriously.

After tea, that same evening, we assembled around the table in the kitchen—the only place where Sailor Ben felt at home—to hear what he had to say for himself.

The candles were snuffed, and a pitcher of foaming nut-brown ale was set at the elbow of the speaker, who was evidently embarrassed by the respectability of his audience, consisting of Captain Nutter, Miss Abigail, myself, and Kitty, whose face shone with happiness like one of the polished tin platters on the dresser.

"Well, my hearties," commenced Sailor Ben—then he stopped short and turned very red, as it struck him that maybe this was not quite the proper way to address a dignitary like the Captain and a severe elderly lady like Miss Abigail Nutter, who sat bolt upright staring at him as she would have stared at the Tycoon of Japan himself.

"I ain't much of a hand at spinnin' a yarn," remarked

Sailor Ben, apologetically, "'specially when the yarn is all about a man as has made a fool of hisself, an' 'specially when that man's name is Benjamin Watson."

"Bravo!" cried Captain Nutter, rapping on the table encouragingly.

"Thankee, sir, thankee. I go back to the time when Kitty an' me was livin' in lodgin's by the dock in New York. We was as happy, sir, as two porpusses, which they toil not neither do they spin. But when I seed the money gittin' low in the locker—Kitty's starboard stockin', savin' your presence, marm—I got downhearted like, seein' as I should be obleeged to ship agin, for it didn't seem as I could do much ashore. An' then the sea was my nat'ral spear of action. I wasn't exactly born on it, look you, but I fell into it the fust time I was let out arter my birth. My mother slipped her cable for a heavenly port afore I was old enough to hail her; so I larnt to look on the ocean for a sort of stepmother—an' a precious hard one she has been to me.

"The idee of leavin' Kitty so soon arter our marriage went agin my grain considerable. I cruised along the docks for somethin' to do in the way of stevedore: an' though I picked up a stray job here and there, I didn't arn enough to buy ship bisket for a rat, let alone feedin' two human mouths. There wasn't nothin' honest I wouldn't have turned a hand to; but the longshoremen gobbled up all the work, an' a outsider like me didn't stand a show.

"Things got from bad to worse; the month's rent took all our cash except a dollar or so, an' the sky looked kind o' squally fore an' aft. Well, I set out one mornin'—that identical unlucky mornin'—determined to come back an' toss some pay into Kitty's lap, if I had to sell my jacket for it. I spied a brig unloadin' coal at pier No. 47—how well I remembers it! I hailed the mate, an' offered myself for a coal-heaver. But I wasn't wanted, as he told me civilly enough, which was better treatment than usual. As I turned off rather glum I was signaled by one of them sleek, smooth-spoken rascals with a white hat an' a weed on it, as is always goin' about the piers a-seekin' who they may devower.

"We sailors know 'em for rascals from stem to starn, but somehow every fresh one fleeces us jest as his mate did afore him. We don't larn nothin' by exper'ence; we're jest no better than a lot of babbys with no brains.

" 'Good mornin', my man,' sez the chap, as iley as you please.

" 'Mornin', sir,' sez I.

" 'Lookin' for a job?' sez he.

" 'Through the big end of a telescope,' sez I—meanin' that the chances for a job looked very small from my pint of view.

" 'You're the man for my money,' sez the sharper, smilin' as innocent as a cherubim; 'jest step in here, till we talk it over.'

"So I goes with him, like a nat'ral-born idiot, into a little grocery shop near by, where we sets down at a table with a bottle atween us. Then it comes out as there is a New Bedford whaler about to start for the fishin' grounds, an' jest one able-bodied sailor like me is wanted to make up the crew. Would I go? Yes, I wouldn't, on no terms.

" 'I'll bet you fifty dollars,' sez he, 'that you'll come back fust mate.'

" 'I'll bet you a hundred,' sez I, 'that I don't, for I've

signed papers as keeps me ashore, an' the parson has
witnessed the deed.'

"So we sat there, he urgin' me to ship, an' I chaffin' him
cheerful over the bottle.

"Arter awhile I begun to feel a little queer; things got
foggy in my upper works, an' I remembers, faint-like, of
signin' a paper; then I remembers bein' in a small boat;
an' then I remembers nothin' until I heard the mate's
whistle pipin' all hands on deck. I tumbled up with the
rest, an' there I was—on board of a whaler outward bound
for a three years' cruise, an' my dear little lass ashore
awaitin' for me."

"Miserable wretch!" said Miss Abigail, in a voice that
vibrated among the tin platters on the dresser. This was
Miss Abigail's way of testifying her sympathy.

"Thankee, marm," returned Sailor Ben, doubtfully.

"No talking to the man at the wheel," cried the Captain. Upon which we all laughed. "Spin!" added my grandfather.

Sailor Ben resumed:

"I leave you to guess the wretchedness as fell upon me, for I've not got the gift to tell you. There I was down on the ship's books for a three years' viage, an' no help for it. I feel nigh to six hundred years old when I think how long that viage was. There isn't no hourglass as runs slow enough to keep a tally of the slowness of them fust hours. But I done my duty like a man, seein' there wasn't no way of gittin' out of it. I told my shipmates of the trick as had been played on me, an' they tried to cheer me up a bit; but I was sore sorrowful for a long spell. Many a night on watch I put my face in my hands and sobbed for thinkin' of the little woman left among the land sharks, an' no man to have an eye on her, God bless her!"

Here Kitty softly drew her chair nearer to Sailor Ben, and rested one hand on his arm.

"Our adventures among the whales, I take it, doesn't consarn the present company here assembled. So I give that the go by. There's an end to everythin', even to a whalin' viage. My heart all but choked me the day we put into New Bedford with our cargo of ile. I got my three years' pay in a lump, an' made for New York like a flash of lightnin'. The people hove to and looked at me, as I rushed through the streets like a madman, until I came to the spot where the lodgin'-house stood on South Street. But, Lord luv ye, there wasn't no sech lodgin'-house there, but a great new brick shop.

"I made bold to go in an' ask arter the old place, but

nobody knowed nothin' about it, save as it had been torn down two years or more. I *was* adrift now, for I had reckoned all them days and nights on gittin' word of Kitty from Dan Shackford, the man as kept the lodgin'.

"As I stood there, with all the wind knocked out of my sails, the idee of runnin' alongside the perlice station popped into my head. The perlice was likely to know the latitude of a man like Dan Shackford, who wasn't over an' above respecktible. They did know—he had died in the Tombs jail that day twelvemonth. A coincydunce, wasn't it? I was ready to drop when they told me this; howsomever, I bore up an' give the chief a notion of the fix I was in. He writ a notice which I put into the newspapers every day for three months; but nothin' come of it. I cruised over the city week in and week out; I went to every sort of place where they hired women hands; I didn't leave a think undone that a uneddicated man could do. But nothin' come of it. I don't believe there was a wretcheder soul in that big city of wretchedness than me. Sometimes I wanted to lay down in the streets and die.

"Driftin' disconsolate one day among the shippin', who should I overhaul but the identical smooth-spoken chap with the white hat an' a weed on it! I didn't know if there was any sperit left in me, till I clapped eye on his very onpleasant countenance. 'You villain!' sez I, 'where's my little Irish lass as you dragged me away from?' an' I lighted on him, hat and all, like that!"

Here Sailor Ben brought his fist down on the deal table with the force of a sledge-hammer. Miss Abigail gave a start, and the ale leaped up in the pitcher like a miniature fountain.

"I begs your parden, ladies and gentlemen all; but the

thought of that feller with his ring an' his watch chain an' his walrus face, is alus too many for me. I was for pitchin' him into the North River, when a perliceman prevented me from benefitin' the human family. I had to pay five dollars for hittin' the chap (they said it was salt an' buttery), an' that's what I call a neat, genteel luxury. It was worth double the money jest to see that white hat, with a weed on it, layin' on the wharf like a busted accordiun.

"Arter months of useless sarch, I went to sea agin. I never got into a foren port but I kept a watch out for Kitty. Once I thought I seed her in Liverpool, but it was only a gal as looked like her. The numbers of women in different parts of the world as looked like her was amazin'. So a good many years crawled by, an' I wandered from place to place, never givin' up the sarch. I might have been chief mate scores of times, maybe master; but I hadn't no ambition. I seed many strange things in them years—outlandish people an' cities, storms, shipwracks, an' battles. I seed many a true mate go down, an' sometimes I envied them what went to their rest. But these things is neither here nor there.

"About a year ago I shipped on board the *Bellephoebe* yonder, an' of all the strange winds as ever blowed, the strangest an' the best was the wind as blowed me to this here blessed spot. I can't be too thankful. That I'm as thankful as it is possible for an uneddicated man to be, He knows as reads the hearts of all."

Here ended Sailor Ben's yarn, which I have written down in his own homely words as nearly as I can recall them. After he had finished, the Captain shook hands with him and served out the ale.

It was a pleasant sight to see the two old lovers sitting side by side, in spite of all, drinking from the same little cup—a battered zinc dipper which Sailor Ben had unslung from a strap round his waist. I think I never saw him without this dipper and a sheath knife suspended just back of his hip, ready for any convivial occasion.

We had a merry time of it. The Captain was in great force this evening, and not only related his famous exploit in the war of 1812, but regaled the company with a dashing sea-song from Mr. Shakespeare's play of *The Tempest*. He had a mellow tenor voice (not Shakespeare, but the Captain), and rolled out the verse with a will:

"The master, the swabber, the boatswain, and I,
    The gunner, and his mate,
Lov'd Mall, Meg, and Marian, and Margery,
    But none of us car'd for Kate."

"A very good song and very well sung," says Sailor Ben; "but some of us *does* care for Kate. Is this Mr. Shawkspear a seafarin' man, sir?"

"Not at present," replied the Captain, with a monstrous twinkle in his eye.

The clock was striking ten when the party broke up. The Captain walked to the "Mariner's Home" with his guest, in order to question him regarding his future movements.

"Well, sir," said he, "I ain't as young as I was, an' I don't cal'ulate to go to sea no more. I proposes to drop anchor here, an' hug the land until the old hulk goes to pieces. I've got two or three thousand dollars in the locker, an' expects to git on uncommon comfortable without askin' no odds from the Assylum for Decayed Mariners."

My grandfather indorsed the plan warmly, and Sailor
Ben did drop anchor in Rivermouth, where he speedily
became one of the institutions of the town.

His first step was to buy a small one-story cottage
located at the head of the wharf, within gunshot of the
Nutter House. To the great amusement of my grandfather, Sailor Ben painted the cottage a light sky-blue,
and ran a broad black stripe around it just under the
eaves. In this stripe he painted white port-holes, at regular distances, making his residence look as much like a
man-of-war as possible. With a short flagstaff projecting
over the door like a bowsprit, the effect was quite magical.
My description of the exterior of this palatial residence is
complete when I add that the proprietor nailed a horse-
shoe against the front door to keep off the witches—a very
necessary precaution in these latitudes.

The inside of Sailor Ben's abode was not less striking
than the outside. The cottage contained two rooms: the
one opening on the wharf he called his cabin; here he ate
and slept. His few tumblers and a frugal collection of
crockery were set in a rack suspended over the table,
which had a cleat of wood nailed round the edge to prevent
the dishes from sliding off in case of a heavy sea. Hanging
against the walls were three or four highly colored prints
of celebrated frigates, and a lithograph picture of a
young woman insufficiently clad in the American flag.
This was labeled "Kitty," though I'm sure it looked no
more like her than I did. A walrus tooth with an Eskimo
engraved on it, a shark's jaw, and the blade of a sword-
fish were among the enviable decorations of this apartment. In one corner stood his bunk, or bed, and in the
other his well-worn sea chest, a perfect Pandora's box of

mysteries. You would have thought yourself in the cabin of a real ship.

The little room aft, separated from the cabin by a sliding door, was the caboose. It held a cooking stove, pots, pans, and groceries; also a lot of fishing lines and coils of tarred twine, which made the place smell like a forecastle, and a delightful smell it is—to those who fancy it.

Kitty didn't leave our service, but played housekeeper for both establishments, returning at night to Sailor Ben's. He shortly added a wherry to his worldly goods, and in the fishing season made a very handsome income. During the winter he employed himself manufacturing crab nets, for which he found no lack of customers.

His popularity among the boys was immense. A jack-knife in his expert hand was a whole chest of tools. He could whittle out anything from a wooden chain to a Chinese pagoda, or a full-rigged seventy-four a foot long. To own a ship of Sailor Ben's building was to be exalted above your fellow creatures. He didn't carve many, and those he refused to sell, choosing to present them to his young friends, of whom Tom Bailey, you may be sure, was one.

How delightful it was of winter nights to sit in his cosy cabin, close to the ship's stove (he wouldn't hear of having a fireplace), and listen to Sailor Ben's yarns! In the early summer twilights, when he sat on the doorstep splicing a rope or mending a net, he always had a bevy of blooming young faces alongside.

The dear old fellow! How tenderly the years touched him after this!—all the more tenderly, it seemed, for having roughed him so cruelly in other days.

SEVENTEEN

HOW WE ASTONISHED THE

RIVERMOUTHIANS

SAILOR BEN'S arrival partly drove the New Orleans project from my brain. Besides, there was just then a certain movement on foot by the Centipede Club which helped to engross my attention.

Pepper Whitcomb took the Captain's veto philosophically, observing that he thought from the first the governor wouldn't let me go. I don't think Pepper was quite honest in that. But to the subject in hand.

Among the few changes that have taken place in Rivermouth during the past twenty years there is one which I regret. I lament the removal of all those varnished iron cannon which used to do duty as posts at the corners of

streets leading from the river. They were quaintly orna-
mental, each set upon end with a solid shot soldered into
its mouth, and gave to that part of the town a pictur-
esqueness very poorly atoned for by the conventional
wooden stakes that have deposed them.

These guns ("old sogers" the boys called them) had
their story, like everything else in Rivermouth. When that
everlasting last war—the war of 1812, I mean—came to
an end, all the brigs, schooners, and barks fitted out at
this port as privateers were as eager to get rid of their
useless twelve-pounders and swivels as they had previously
been to obtain them. Many of the pieces had cost large
sums, and now they were little better than so much crude
iron—not so good, in fact, for they were clumsy things to
break up and melt over. The government didn't want
them; private citizens didn't want them; they were a drug
in the market.

But there was one man, ridiculous beyond his generation, who got it into his head that a fortune was to be
made out of these same guns. To buy them all, to hold
onto them until war was declared again (as he had no
doubt it would be in a few months), and then sell out at
fabulous prices—this was the daring idea that addled the
pate of Silas Trefethen, "Dealer in E. & W. I. Goods and
Groceries," as the faded sign over his shop door informed
the public.

Silas went shrewdly to work, buying up every old cannon he could lay hands on. His backyard was soon
crowded with broken-down gun carriages, and his barn
with guns, like an arsenal. When Silas's purpose got wind
it was astonishing how valuable that thing became which
just now was worth nothing at all.

"Ha, ha!" thought Silas; "somebody else is tryin' tu git control of the market. But I guess I've got the start of *him*."

So he went on buying and buying, oftentimes paying double the original price of the article. People in the neighboring towns collected all the worthless ordnance they could find, and sent it by the cartload to Rivermouth.

When his barn was full, Silas began piling the rubbish in his cellar, then in his parlor. He mortgaged the stock of his grocery store, mortgaged his house, his barn, his horse, and would have mortgaged himself, if any one would have taken him as security, in order to carry on the grand speculation. He was a ruined man, and as happy as a lark.

Surely poor Silas was cracked, like the majority of his own cannon. More or less crazy he must have been always. Years before this he purchased an elegant rosewood coffin, and kept it in one of the spare rooms in his residence. He even had his name engraved on the silver plate, leaving a blank after the word "Died."

The blank was filled up in due time, and well it was for Silas that he secured so stylish a coffin in his opulent days, for when he died his worldly wealth would not have bought him a pine box, to say nothing of rosewood. He never gave up expecting a war with Great Britain. Hopeful and radiant to the last, his dying words were, *England—war —few days—great profits!*

It was that sweet old lady, Dame Jocelyn, who told me the story of Silas Trefethen; for these things happened long before my day. Silas died in 1817.

At Trefethen's death his unique collection came under the auctioneer's hammer. Some of the larger guns were sold to the town, and planted at the corners of divers streets; others went off to the iron foundry; the balance, numbering twelve, were dumped down on a deserted wharf at the foot of Anchor Lane, where, summer after summer, they rested at their ease in the grass and fungi, pelted in autumn by the rain, and annually buried by the winter snow. It is with these twelve guns that our story has to deal.

The wharf where they reposed was shut off from the street by a high fence—a silent, dreamy old wharf, covered with strange weeds and mosses. On account of its seclusion and the good fishing it afforded, it was much frequented by us boys.

There we met many an afternoon to throw out our lines, or play leap frog among the rusty cannon. They were famous fellows in our eyes. What a racket they had made in the heyday of their unchastened youth! What stories they might tell now, if their puffy metallic lips could only speak! Once they were lively talkers enough; but there the grim sea-dogs lay, silent and forlorn in spite of all their former growlings.

They always seemed to me like a lot of venerable disabled tars, stretched out on a lawn in front of a hospital, gazing seaward, and mutely lamenting their lost youth.

But once more they were destined to lift up their dolorous voices—once more ere they keeled over and lay speechless for all time. And this is how it befell.

Jack Harris, Charley Marden, Harry Blake, and myself were fishing off the grass-grown wharf one afternoon, when a thought flashed upon me like an inspiration.

"I say, boys!" I cried, hauling in my line hand over hand, "I've got something!"

"What does it pull like, youngster?" asked Harris, looking down at the taut line and expecting to see a big perch at last.

"Oh, nothing in the fish way," I returned, laughing; "it's about the old guns."

"What about them?"

"I was thinking what jolly fun it would be to set one of the old sogers on his legs and serve him out a ration of gunpowder."

Up came the three lines in a jiffy. An enterprise better suited to the disposition of my companions could not have been proposed.

In a short time we had one of the smaller cannon over on its back and were busy scraping the green rust from the touch-hole. The mould had spiked the gun so effectually, that for a while we fancied we should have to give up our attempt to resuscitate the old soger.

"A long gimlet would clear it out," said Charley Marden, "if we only had one."

I looked to see if Sailor Ben's flag was flying at the cabin door, for he always took in the colors when he went off fishing.

"When you want to know if the Admiral's abroad, jest cast an eye to the buntin', my hearties," says Sailor Ben.

Sometimes in a jocose mood he called himself the Admiral, and I am sure he deserved to be one. The Admiral's flag was flying, and I soon procured a gimlet from his carefully kept toolchest.

Before long we had the gun in working order. A newspaper lashed to the end of a lath served as a swab to dust out the bore. Jack Harris blew through the touch-hole and pronounced all clear.

Seeing our task accomplished so easily, we turned our attention to the other guns, which lay in all sorts of postures in the rank grass. Borrowing a rope from Sailor Ben, we managed with immense labor to drag the heavy pieces into position and place a brick under each muzzle to give it the proper elevation. When we beheld them all in a row, like a regular battery, we simultaneously conceived an idea, the magnitude of which struck us dumb for a moment.

Our first intention was to load and fire a single gun. How feeble and insignificant was such a plan compared to that which now sent the light dancing into our eyes!

"What could we have been thinking of?" cried Jack Harris. "We'll give 'em a broadside, to be sure, if we die for it!"

We turned to with a will, and before nightfall had nearly half the battery overhauled and ready for service. To keep the artillery dry we stuffed wads of loose hemp into the muzzles, and fitted wooden pegs to the touchholes.

At recess the next noon the Centipedes met in a corner of the schoolyard to talk over the proposed lark. The original projectors, though they would have liked to keep the thing secret, were obliged to make a club matter of it, inasmuch as funds were required for ammunition. There had been no recent drain on the treasury, and the society could well afford to spend a few dollars in so notable an undertaking.

It was unanimously agreed that the plan should be carried out in the handsomest manner, and a subscription to that end was taken on the spot. Several of the Centipedes hadn't a cent, excepting the one strung around their necks; others, however, were richer. I chanced to

HOW WE ASTONISHED THE RIVERMOUTHIANS 175

have a dollar, and it went into the cap quicker than lightning. When the club, in view of my munificence, voted to
name the guns Bailey's Battery I was prouder than I
have ever been since over anything.

The money thus raised, added to that already in the
treasury, amounted to nine dollars—a fortune in those
days; but not more than we had use for. This sum was
divided into twelve parts, for it would not do for one boy
to buy all the powder, nor even for us all to make our
purchases at the same place. That would excite suspicion
at any time, particularly at a period so remote from the
Fourth of July.

There were only three stores in town licensed to sell
powder; that gave each store four customers. Not to run
the slightest risk of remark, one boy bought his powder
on Monday, the next boy on Tuesday, and so on until
the requisite quantity was in our possession. This we put
into a keg and carefully hid in a dry spot on the wharf.

Our next step was to finish cleaning the guns, which
occupied two afternoons, for several of the old sogers
were in a very congested state indeed. Having completed
the task, we came upon a difficulty. To set off the battery
by daylight was out of the question; it must be done at
night; it must be done with fuses, for no doubt the neighbors would turn out after the first two or three shots, and
it would not pay to be caught in the vicinity.

Who knew anything about fuses? Who could arrange
it so the guns would go off one after the other, with an
interval of a minute or so between?

Theoretically we knew that a minute-fuse lasted a minute; double the quantity, two minutes; but practically we
were at a standstill. There was but one person who could

help us in this extremity—Sailor Ben. To me was assigned
the duty of obtaining what information I could from the
ex-gunner, it being left to my discretion whether or not
to intrust him with our secret.

So one evening I dropped into the cabin and artfully
turned the conversation to fuses in general, and then to
particular fuses, but without getting much out of the
old boy, who was busy making a twine hammock. Finally,
I was forced to divulge the whole plot.

The Admiral had a sailor's love for a joke, and entered
at once and heartily into our scheme. He volunteered to
prepare the fuses himself, and I left the labor in his hands,
having bound him by several extraordinary oaths—such
as "Hope-I-may-die" and "Shiver-my-timbers"—not to
betray us, come what would.

This was Monday evening. On Wednesday the fuses
were ready. That night we were to unmuzzle Bailey's
Battery. Mr. Grimshaw saw that something was wrong
somewhere, for we were restless and absentminded in the
classes, and the best of us came to grief before the morning session was over. When Mr. Grimshaw announced
"Guy Fawkes" as the subject for our next composition,
you might have knocked down the Mystic Twelve with a
feather.

The coincidence was certainly curious, but when a man
has committed, or is about to commit, an offense, a hundred trifles, which would pass unnoticed at another time,
seem to point at him with convicting fingers. No doubt
Guy Fawkes himself received many a start after he had
got his wicked kegs of gunpowder neatly piled up under
the House of Lords.

Wednesday, as I have mentioned, was a half-holiday,

and the Centipedes assembled in my barn to decide on the final arrangements. These were as simple as could be. As the fuses were connected, it needed but one person to fire the train. Hereupon arose a discussion as to who was the proper person. Some argued that I ought to apply the match, the battery being christened after me, and the main idea, moreover, being mine. Others advocated the claim of Phil Adams as the oldest boy. At last we drew lots for the post of honor.

Twelve slips of folded paper, upon one of which was written "Thou art the man," were placed in a quart measure, and thoroughly shaken; then each member stepped up and lifted out his destiny. At a given signal we opened our billets. "Thou art the man," said the slip of paper trembling in my fingers. The sweets and anxieties of a leader were mine the rest of the afternoon.

Directly after twilight set in Phil Adams stole down to the wharf and fixed the fuses to the guns, laying a train of powder from the principal fuse to the fence, through a chink of which I was to drop the match at midnight.

At ten o'clock Rivermouth goes to bed.

At eleven o'clock Rivermouth is as quiet as a country churchyard.

At twelve o'clock there is nothing left with which to compare the stillness that broods over the little seaport.

In the midst of this stillness I arose and glided out of the house like a phantom bent on an evil errand; like a phantom I flitted through the silent street, hardly drawing breath until I knelt down beside the fence at the appointed place.

Pausing a moment for my heart to stop thumping, I lighted the match and shielded it with both hands until it was well under way, and then dropped the blazing splinter on the slender thread of gunpowder.

A noiseless flash instantly followed, and all was dark again. I peeped through the crevice in the fence, and saw the main fuse spitting out sparks like a conjurer. Assured that the train had not failed, I took to my heels, fearful lest the fuse might burn more rapidly than we calculated, and cause an explosion before I could get home. This, luckily, did not happen. There's a special Providence that watches over idiots, drunken men, and boys.

I dodged the ceremony of undressing by plunging into bed, jacket, boots, and all. I am not sure I took off my cap; but I know that I had hardly pulled the coverlid over me, when "Boom!" sounded the first gun of Bailey's Battery.

I lay as still as a mouse. In less than two minutes there was another burst of thunder, and then another. The third gun was a tremendous fellow and fairly shook the house.

The town was waking up. Windows were thrown open here and there and people called to each other across the streets asking what that firing was for.

"Boom!" went gun number four.

I sprung out of bed and tore off my jacket, for I heard the Captain feeling his way along the wall to my chamber. I was half undressed by the time he found the knob of the door.

"I say, sir," I cried, "do you hear those guns?"

"Not being deaf, I do," said the Captain, a little tartly —any reflection on his hearing always nettled him; "but what on earth they are for I can't conceive. You had better get up and dress yourself."

"I'm nearly dressed, sir."

"Boom! boom!"—two of the guns had gone off together.

The door of Miss Abigail's bedroom opened hastily, and that pink of maidenly propriety stepped out into the hall in her nightgown—the only indecorous thing I ever knew her to do. She held a lighted candle in her hand and looked like a very aged Lady Macbeth.

"O Dan'el, this is dreadful! What do you suppose it means?"

"I really can't suppose," said the Captain, rubbing his ear; "but I guess it's over now."

"Boom!" said Bailey's Battery.

Rivermouth was wide awake now, and half the male population were in the streets, running different ways, for the firing seemed to proceed from opposite points of the town. Everybody waylaid everybody else with questions; but as no one knew what was the occasion of the tumult, people who were not usually nervous began to be oppressed by the mystery.

Some thought the town was being bombarded; some thought the world was coming to an end, as the pious and ingenious Mr. Miller had predicted it would; but those who couldn't form any theory whatever were the most perplexed.

In the meanwhile Bailey's Battery bellowed away at regular intervals. The greatest confusion reigned everywhere by this time. People with lanterns rushed hither and thither. The town watch had turned out to a man, and marched off, in admirable order, in the wrong direction. Discovering their mistake, they retraced their steps, and got down to the wharf just as the last cannon belched forth its lightning.

A dense cloud of sulphurous smoke floated over Anchor Lane, obscuring the starlight. Two or three hundred people, in various stages of excitement, crowded about the upper end of the wharf, not liking to advance farther until they were satisfied that the explosions were over.

A board was here and there blown from the fence, and through the openings thus afforded a few of the more daring spirits at length ventured to crawl.

The cause of the racket soon transpired. A suspicion that they had been sold gradually dawned on the River-mouthians. Many were exceedingly indignant, and declared that no penalty was severe enough for those concerned in such a prank; others—and these were the very people who had been terrified nearly out of their wits—had the assurance to laugh, saying that they knew all along it was only a trick.

The town watch boldly took possession of the ground, and the crowd began to disperse. Knots of gossips lingered here and there near the place, indulging in vain surmises as to who the invisible gunners could be.

There was no more noise that night, but many a timid person lay awake expecting a renewal of the mysterious cannonading. The Oldest Inhabitant refused to go to bed on any terms, but persisted in sitting up in a rocking chair, with his hat and mittens on, until daybreak.

I thought I should never get to sleep. The moment I drifted off in a doze I fell to laughing and woke myself up. But towards morning slumber overtook me, and I had a series of disagreeable dreams, in one of which I was waited upon by the ghost of Silas Trefethen with an exorbitant bill for the use of his guns. In another, I was dragged before a court-martial and sentenced by Sailor Ben, in a frizzled wig and three-cornered cocked hat, to be shot to death by Bailey's Battery—a sentence which Sailor Ben was about to execute with his own hand, when I suddenly opened my eyes and found the sunshine lying pleasantly across my face. I tell you I was glad!

That unaccountable fascination which leads the guilty to hover about the spot where his crime was committed drew me down to the wharf as soon as I was dressed. Phil Adams, Jack Harris, and others of the conspirators were already there, examining with a mingled feeling of curiosity and apprehension the havoc accomplished by the battery.

The fence was badly shattered and the ground ploughed up for several yards round the place where the guns formerly lay—formerly lay, for now they were scattered every which way. There was scarcely a gun that hadn't burst. Here was one ripped open from muzzle to breech, and there was another with its mouth blown into the shape of a trumpet. Three of the guns had disappeared bodily, but on looking over the edge of the wharf we saw them standing on end in the tide mud. They had popped overboard in their excitement.

"I tell you what, fellows," whispered Phil Adams, "it is lucky we didn't try to touch 'em off with punk. They'd have blown us all to flinders."

The destruction of Bailey's Battery was not, unfortunately, the only catastrophe. A fragment of one of the cannon had carried away the chimney of Sailor Ben's cabin. He was very mad at first, but having prepared the fuse himself he didn't dare complain openly.

"I'd have taken a reef in the blessed stovepipe," said the Admiral, gazing ruefully at the smashed chimney, "if I had known as how the Flagship was agoin' to be under fire."

The next day he rigged out an iron funnel, which, being in sections, could be detached and taken in at a moment's notice. On the whole, I think he inwardly gloated over the demolition of his brick chimney. The stovepipe was a great deal more shipshape.

The town was not so easily appeased. The selectmen determined to make an example of the guilty parties, and offered a reward for their arrest, holding out a promise of pardon to any one of the offenders who would furnish information against the rest. But there were no faint hearts among the Centipedes. Suspicion rested for a while on several persons—on the soldiers at the fort; on a crazy fellow, known about town as "Bottle-Nose"; and at last on Sailor Ben.

"Shiver my timbers!" cries that deeply injured individual. "Do you suppose, sir, as I have lived to sixty year, an' ain't got no more sense than to go for to blaze away at my own upper riggin'? It doesn't stand to reason."

It certainly did not seem probable that Mr. Watson would maliciously knock over his own chimney, and Lawyer Scratch, who had the case in hand, bowed himself out of the Admiral's cabin convinced that the right man had not been discovered.

People living by the sea are always more or less superstitious. Stories of specter ships and mysterious beacons, that lure vessels out of their course and wreck them on unknown reefs, were among the stock legends of Rivermouth; and not a few people in the town were ready to attribute the firing of those guns to some supernatural agency. The Oldest Inhabitant remembered that when he was a boy a dim-looking sort of schooner hove to in the offing one foggy afternoon, fired off a single gun that didn't make any report, and then crumbled to nothing, spar, mast, and hulk, like a piece of burnt paper.

The authorities, however, were of the opinion that human hands had something to do with the explosions, and they resorted to deep-laid stratagems to get hold of the said hands. One of their traps came very near catching us. They artfully caused an old brass field piece to be left on a wharf near the scene of our late operations. Nothing in the world but the lack of money to buy powder saved us from falling into the clutches of the two watchmen who lay secreted for a week in a neighboring sail loft.

It was many a day before the midnight bombardment ceased to be the town talk. The trick was so audacious and on so grand a scale that nobody thought for an instant of connecting us lads with it. Suspicion at length grew weary of lighting on the wrong person, and as conjecture—like the physicians in the epitaph—was in vain, the Rivermouthians gave up the idea of finding out who had astonished them.

They never did find out, and never will, unless they read this veracious history. If the selectmen are still disposed to punish the malefactors, I can supply Lawyer Scratch with evidence enough to convict Pepper Whitcomb, Phil Adams, Charley Marden, and the other honorable members of the Centipede Club. But really I don't think it would pay now.

EIGHTEEN

A FROG HE WOULD A-WOOING GO

IF THE reader supposes that I lived all this while in Rivermouth without falling a victim to one or more of the young ladies attending Miss Dorothy Gibbs's Female Institute, why, then, all I have to say is the reader exhibits his ignorance of human nature.

Miss Gibbs's seminary was located within a few minutes' walk of the Temple Grammar School, and numbered about thirty-five pupils, the majority of whom boarded at the Hall—Primrose Hall, as Miss Dorothy prettily called it. The Primroses, as we called *them*, ranged from seven years of age to sweet seventeen, and a prettier group of sirens never got together even in Rivermouth, for Rivermouth, you should know, is famous for its pretty girls.

There were tall girls and short girls, rosy girls and pale girls, and girls as brown as berries; girls like Amazons, slender girls, weird and winning like Undine, girls

185

with black tresses, girls with auburn ringlets, girls with
every tinge of golden hair. To behold Miss Dorothy's
young ladies of a Sunday morning walking to church two
by two, the smallest toddling at the end of the procession
like the bobs at the tail of a kite, was a spectacle to fill
with tender emotion the least susceptible heart. To see
Miss Dorothy marching grimly at the head of her light
infantry, was to feel the hopelessness of making an attack
on any part of the column.

She was a perfect dragon of watchfulness. The most
unguarded lifting of an eyelash in the fluttering battalion
was sufficient to put her on the lookout. She had had experiences with the male sex, this Miss Dorothy so prim
and grim. It was whispered that her heart was a tattered
album scrawled over with love lines, but that she had shut
up the volume long ago.

There was a tradition that she had been crossed in love;
but it was the faintest of traditions. A gay young lieutenant of marines had flirted with her at a country ball (A.D.
1811), and then marched carelessly away at the head of
his company to the shrill music of the fife, without so much
as a sigh for the girl he left behind him. The years rolled
on, the gallant gay Lothario—which wasn't his name—
married, became a father, and then a grandfather; and
at the period of which I am speaking his grandchild was
actually one of Miss Dorothy's young ladies. So, at least,
ran the story.

The lieutenant himself was dead these many years; but
Miss Dorothy never got over his duplicity. She was convinced that the sole aim of mankind was to win the unguarded affection of maidens, and then march off treach-
erously with flying colors to the heartless music of the

drum and fife. To shield the inmates of Primrose Hall
from the bitter influences that had blighted her own early
affections was Miss Dorothy's mission in life.

"No wolves prowling about my lambs, if *you* please,"
said Miss Dorothy. "I will not allow it."

She was as good as her word. I don't think the boy lives
who ever set foot within the limits of Primrose Hall while
the seminary was under her charge. Perhaps if Miss Dorothy had given her young ladies a little more liberty, they
would not have thought it "such fun" to make eyes over
the white lattice fence at the young gentlemen of the
Temple Grammar School. I say perhaps; for it is one
thing to manage thirty-five young ladies and quite another thing to talk about it.

But all Miss Dorothy's vigilance could not prevent the
young folks from meeting in the town now and then, nor
could her utmost ingenuity interrupt postal arrangements. There was no end of notes passing between the
students and the Primroses. Notes tied to the heads of
arrows were shot into dormitory windows; notes were
tucked under fences, and hidden in the trunks of decayed
trees. Every thick place in the boxwood hedge that surrounded the seminary was a possible post office.

It was a terrible shock to Miss Dorothy the day she unearthed a nest of letters in one of the huge wooden urns
surmounting the gateway that led to her dovecot. It was
a bitter moment to Miss Phoebe and Miss Candace and
Miss Hesba, when they had their locks of hair grimly
handed back to them by Miss Gibbs in the presence of the
whole school. Girls whose locks of hair had run the block-
ade in safety were particularly severe on the offenders.
But it didn't stop other notes and other tresses, and I

would like to know what can stop them while the earth holds together.

Now when I first came to Rivermouth I looked upon girls as rather tame company; I hadn't a spark of sentiment concerning them; but seeing my comrades sending and receiving mysterious epistles, wearing bits of ribbon in their buttonholes and leaving packages of confectionery (generally lemon drops) in the hollow trunks of trees— why, I felt that this was the proper thing to do. I resolved, as a matter of duty, to fall in love with somebody, and I didn't care in the least who it was. In much the same mood that Don Quixote selected the Dulcinea del Toboso for his lady love, I singled out one of Miss Dorothy's incomparable young ladies for mine.

I debated a long while whether I should not select *two*, but at last settled down on one—a pale little girl with blue eyes, named Alice. I shall not make a long story of this, for Alice made short work of me. She was secretly in love with Pepper Whitcomb. This occasioned a temporary coolness between Pepper and myself.

Not disheartened, however, I placed Laura Rice—I believe it was Laura Rice—in the vacant niche. The new idol was more cruel than the old. The former frankly sent me to the right about, but the latter was a deceitful lot. She wore my nosegay in her dress at the evening service (the Primroses were marched to church three times every Sunday), she penned me the daintiest of notes, she sent me the glossiest of ringlets (cut, as I afterwards found out, from the stupid head of Miss Gibbs's chambermaid), and at the same time was holding me and my pony up to ridicule in a series of letters written to Jack Harris. It was Harris himself who kindly opened my eyes.

"I tell you what, Bailey," said that young gentleman, "Laura is an old veteran, and carries too many guns for a youngster. She can't resist a flirtation; I believe she'd flirt with an infant in arms. There's hardly a fellow in the school that hasn't worn her colors and some of her hair. She doesn't give out any more of her own hair now. It's been pretty well used up. The demand was greater than the supply, you see. It's all very well to correspond with Laura, but as to looking for anything serious from her, the knowing ones don't. Hope I haven't hurt your feelings, old boy," (that was a soothing stroke of flattery to call me "old boy,") "but 'twas my duty as a friend and a Centipede to let you know who you were dealing with."

Such was the advice given me by that time-stricken, careworn, and embittered man of the world, who was sixteen years old if he was a day.

I dropped Laura. In the course of the next twelve months I had perhaps three or four similar experiences, and the conclusion was forced upon me that I was not a boy likely to distinguish myself in this branch of business.

I fought shy of Primrose Hall from that moment. Smiles were smiled over the boxwood hedge, and little hands were occasionally kissed to me; but I only winked my eye patronizingly, and passed on. I never renewed tender relations with Miss Gibbs's young ladies. All this occurred during my first year and a half at Rivermouth.

Between my studies at school, my outdoor recreations, and the hurts my vanity received, I managed to escape for the time being any very serious attack of that love fever which, like the measles, is almost certain to seize upon a boy sooner or later. I was not to be an exception. I was merely biding my time. The incidents I have now to relate took place shortly after the events described in the last chapter.

In a life so tranquil and circumscribed as ours in the Nutter House, a visitor was a novelty of no little importance. The whole household awoke from its quietude one morning when the Captain announced that a young niece of his from New York was to spend a few weeks with us.

The blue chintz room, into which a ray of sun was never allowed to penetrate, was thrown open and dusted, and its moldy air made sweet with a bouquet of pot roses placed on the old-fashioned bureau. Kitty was busy all the forenoon washing off the sidewalk and sandpapering the great brass knocker on our front door; and Miss Abigail was up to her elbows in a pigeon pie.

I felt sure it was for no ordinary person that all these preparations were in progress; and I was right. Miss Nelly Glentworth was no ordinary person. I shall never believe she was. There may have been lovelier women, though I have never seen them; there may have been more brilliant women, though it has not been my fortune to meet them; but that there was ever a more charming one than Nelly Glentworth is a proposition against which I contend.

I don't love her now. I don't think of her once in five years; and yet it would give me a turn if in the course of my daily walk I should suddenly come upon her eldest boy. I may say that her eldest boy was not playing a prominent part in this life when I first made her acquaintance.

It was a drizzling, cheerless afternoon towards the end of summer that a hack drew up at the door of the Nutter

House. The Captain and Miss Abigail hastened into the hall on hearing the carriage stop. In a moment more Miss Nelly Glentworth was seated in our sitting-room undergoing a critical examination at the hands of a small boy who lounged uncomfortably on a settee between the windows.

The small boy considered himself a judge of girls, and he rapidly came to the following conclusions: that Miss Nelly was about nineteen; that she had not given away much of her back hair, which hung in two massive chestnut braids over her shoulders; that she was a shade too pale and a trifle too tall; that her hands were nicely shaped and her feet much too diminutive for daily use. He furthermore observed that her voice was musical, and that her face lighted up with an indescribable brightness when she smiled.

On the whole, the small boy liked her well enough; and, satisfied that she was not a person to be afraid of, but, on the contrary, one who might be made quite agreeable, he departed to keep an appointment with his friend Sir Pepper Whitcomb.

But the next morning when Miss Glentworth came down to breakfast in a purple dress, her face as fresh as one of the moss roses on the bureau upstairs, and her laugh as contagious as the merriment of a robin, the small boy experienced a strange sensation, and mentally compared her with the loveliest of Miss Gibbs's young ladies, and found those young ladies wanting in the balance.

A night's rest had wrought a wonderful change in Miss Nelly. The pallor and weariness of the journey had passed away. I looked at her through the toast rack and thought I had never seen anything more winning than her smile.

After breakfast she went out with me to the stable to see Gypsy, and the three of us became friends then and there. Nelly was the only girl that Gypsy ever took the slightest notice of.

It chanced to be a half-holiday, and a baseball match of unusual interest was to come off on the school ground that afternoon; but, somehow, I didn't go. I hung about the house abstractedly. The Captain went up town, and Miss Abigail was busy in the kitchen making immortal gingerbread. I drifted into the sitting-room, and had our guest all to myself for I don't know how many hours. It was twilight, I recollect, when the Captain returned with letters for Miss Nelly.

Many a time after that I sat with her through the dreamy September afternoons. If I had played baseball it would have been much better for me.

Those first days of Miss Nelly's visit are very misty in my remembrance. I try in vain to remember just when I began to fall in love with her. Whether the spell worked upon me gradually or fell upon me all at once, I don't know. I only know that it seemed to me as if I had always loved her. Things that took place before she came were dim to me, like events that had occurred in the Middle Ages.

Nelly was at least five years my senior. But what of that? Adam is the only man I ever heard of who didn't in early youth fall in love with a woman older than himself, and I am convinced that he would have done so if he had had the opportunity.

I wonder if girls from fifteen to twenty are aware of the glamour they cast over the straggling, awkward boys whom they regard and treat as mere children? I wonder, now. Young women are so keen in such matters. I wonder if Miss Nelly Glentworth never suspected until the very last night of her visit at Rivermouth that I was over ears in love with her pretty self, and was suffering pangs as poignant as if I had been ten feet high and as old as Methuselah? For, indeed, I was miserable throughout all those five weeks. I went down in the Latin class at the rate of three boys a day. Her fresh young eyes came between me and my book, and there was an end of Virgil.

> O love, love, love!
> Love is like a dizziness,
> It winna let a body
> Gang aboot his business.

I was wretched away from her, and only less wretched in her presence. The especial cause of my woe was this: I was simply a little boy to Miss Glentworth. I knew it. I bewailed it. I ground my teeth and wept in secret over the fact. If I had been aught else in her eyes would she have smoothed my hair so carelessly, sending an electric shock through my whole system? would she have walked with me, hand in hand, for hours in the old garden? and once when I lay on the sofa, my head aching with love and mortification, would she have stooped down and kissed me if I hadn't been a little boy? How I despised little boys! How I hated one particular little boy—too little to be loved!

I smile over this very grimly even now. My sorrow was genuine and bitter. It is a great mistake on the part of elderly ladies, male and female, to tell a child that he is seeing his happiest days. Don't you believe a word of it, my little friend. The burdens of childhood are as hard to bear as the crosses that weigh us down later in life, while the happinesses of childhood are tame compared with those of our maturer years. And even if this were not so, it is rank cruelty to throw shadows over the young heart by croaking, "Be merry, for tomorrow you die!"

As the last days of Nelly's visit drew near, I fell into a very unhealthy state of mind. To have her so frank and unconsciously coquettish with me, was a daily torment; to be looked upon and treated as a child was bitter almonds; but the thought of losing her altogether was distraction.

The summer was at an end. The days were perceptibly shorter, and now and then came an evening when it was chilly enough to have a wood fire in our sitting-room. The leaves were beginning to take hectic tints, and the wind was practising the minor pathetic notes of its autumnal dirge. Nature and myself appeared to be approaching our dissolution simultaneously.

One evening, the evening previous to the day set for Nelly's departure—how well I remember it!—I found her sitting alone by the wide chimneypiece looking musingly at the crackling back log. There were no candles in the room. On her face and hands, and on the small golden cross at her throat, fell the flickering firelight—that ruddy, mellow firelight in which one's grandmother would look poetical.

I drew a low stool from the corner and placed it by the side of her chair. She reached out her hand to me, as was her pretty fashion, and so we sat for several moments silently in the changing glow of the burning logs. At length I moved back the stool so that I could see her face in profile without being seen by her. I lost her hand by this movement, but I couldn't have spoken with the listless touch of her fingers on mine. After two or three attempts I said "Nelly" a good deal louder than I intended.

Perhaps the effort it cost me was evident in my voice. She raised herself quickly in the chair and half turned towards me.

"Well, Tom?"

"I—I am very sorry you are going away."

"So am I. I have enjoyed every hour of my visit."

"Do you think you will ever come back here?"

"Perhaps," said Nelly, and her eyes wandered off into the fitful firelight.

"I suppose you will forget us all very quickly."

"Indeed I shall not. I shall always have the pleasantest memories of Rivermouth."

Here the conversation died a natural death. Nelly sank into a sort of dream, and I meditated. Fearing every moment to be interrupted by some member of the family, I nerved myself to make a bold dash.

"Nelly."

"Well."

"Do you—" I hesitated.

"Do I what?"

"Love anyone very much?"

"Why, of course I do," said Nelly, scattering her revery with a merry laugh. "I love Uncle Nutter, and Aunt Nutter, and you—and Towser."

Towser, our new dog! I couldn't stand that. I pushed back the stool impatiently and stood in front of her.

"That's not what I mean," I said angrily.

"Well, what do you mean?"

"Do you love anyone to marry him?"

"The idea of it!" cried Nelly, laughing.

"But you must tell me!"

"Must, Tom?"

"Indeed you must, Nelly."

She had risen from the chair with an amused, perplexed look in her eyes. I held her an instant by the dress.

"Please tell me, Nelly."

"O you silly boy!" cried Nelly. Then she rumpled my

hair all over my forehead and ran laughing out of the room.

Suppose Cinderella had rumpled the Prince's hair all over *his* forehead, how would he have liked it? Suppose the Sleeping Beauty, when the king's son with a kiss set her and all the old clocks a-going in the spellbound castle —suppose, I say, the young minx had looked up and coolly laughed in his eye, I guess the king's son wouldn't have been greatly pleased.

I hesitated a second or two, and then rushed after Nelly just in time to run against Miss Abigail, who entered the room with a couple of lighted candles.

"Goodness gracious, Tom!" exclaimed Miss Abigail, "*are* you possessed?"

I left her scraping the warm spermaceti from one of her thumbs.

Nelly was in the kitchen talking quite unconcernedly with Kitty Collins. There she remained until suppertime. Supper over, we all adjourned to the sitting-room. I planned and plotted, but could manage in no way to get Nelly alone. She and the Captain played cribbage all the evening.

The next morning my lady did not make her appearance until we were seated at the breakfast table. I had got up at daylight myself. Immediately after breakfast the carriage arrived to take her to the railway station. A gentleman stepped from this carriage, and greatly to my surprise was warmly welcomed by the Captain and Miss Abigail, and by Miss Nelly herself, who seemed unnecessarily glad to see him. From the hasty conversation that followed I learned that the gentleman had come somewhat unexpectedly to conduct Miss Nelly to Boston. But how

did he know that she was to leave that morning? Nelly
bade farewell to the Captain and Miss Abigail, made a
little rush and kissed me on the nose, and was gone.

As the wheels of the hack rolled up the street and over
my finer feelings, I turned to the Captain.

"Who was that gentleman, sir?"

"That was Mr. Waldron."

"A relation of yours, sir?" I asked, craftily.

"No relation of mine—a relation of Nelly's," said the
Captain, smiling.

"A cousin?" I suggested, feeling a strange hatred
spring up in my bosom for the unknown.

"Well, I suppose you might call him a cousin for the
present. He's going to marry little Nelly next summer."

In one of Peter Parley's valuable historical works is a
description of an earthquake at Lisbon. "At the first shock
the inhabitants rushed into the streets; the earth yawned
at their feet and the houses tottered and fell on every
side." I staggered past the Captain into the street; a gid-
diness came over me; the earth yawned at my feet, and the
houses threatened to fall in on every side of me. How
distinctly I remember that momentary sense of confusion
when everything in the world seemed toppling over into
ruins.

As I have remarked, my love for Nelly is a thing of the
past. I had not thought of her for years until I sat down
to write this chapter, and yet, now that all is said and
done, I shouldn't care particularly to come across Mrs.
Waldron's eldest boy in my afternoon's walk. He must be
fourteen or fifteen years old by this time—the young
villain!

I BECOME A BLIGHTED BEING

WHEN a young boy gets to be an old boy, when the hair is growing rather thin on the top of the old boy's head, and he has been tamed sufficiently to take a sort of chastened pleasure in allowing the baby to play with his watch seals—when, I say, an old boy has reached this stage in the journey of life, he is sometimes apt to indulge in sportive remarks concerning his first love.

Now, though I bless my stars that it wasn't in my power to marry Miss Nelly, I am not going to deny my boyish regard for her nor laugh at it. As long as it lasted it was a very sincere and unselfish love, and rendered me proportionately wretched. I say as long as it lasted, for one's first love doesn't last forever.

I am ready, however, to laugh at the amusing figure I cut after I had really ceased to have any deep feeling in the matter. It was then I took it into my head to be a Blighted Being. This was about two weeks after the spectral appearance of Mr. Waldron.

For a boy of a naturally vivacious disposition the part of a blighted being presented difficulties. I had an excellent appetite, I liked society, I liked out-of-door sports, I was fond of handsome clothes. Now all these things were incompatible with the doleful character I was to assume, and I proceeded to cast them from me. I neglected my hair. I avoided my playmates. I frowned abstractedly. I didn't eat as much as was good for me. I took lonely walks. I brooded in solitude. I not only committed to memory the more turgid poems of the late Lord Byron—"Fare thee well, and if forever," &c.—but I became a despondent poet on my own account, and composed a string of "Stanzas to One who will understand them." I think I was a trifle too hopeful on that point; for I came across the verses several years afterwards, and was quite unable to understand them myself.

It was a great comfort to be so perfectly miserable and yet not suffer any. I used to look in the glass and gloat over the amount and variety of mournful expression I could throw into my features. If I caught myself smiling at anything, I cut the smile short with a sigh. The oddest thing about all this is, I never once suspected that I was *not* unhappy. No one, not even Pepper Whitcomb, was more deceived than I.

Among the minor pleasures of being blighted were the interest and perplexity I excited in the simple souls that were thrown in daily contact with me. Pepper especially. I nearly drove him into a corresponding state of mind.

I had from time to time given Pepper slight but impressive hints of my admiration for Some One (this was in the early part of Miss Glentworth's visit); I had also led him to infer that my admiration was not altogether in vain. He was therefore unable to explain the cause of my strange behavior, for I had carefully refrained from mentioning to Pepper the fact that Some One had turned out to be Another's!

I treated Pepper shabbily. I couldn't resist playing on his tenderer feelings. He was a boy bubbling over with sympathy for anyone in any kind of trouble. Our intimacy since Binny Wallace's death had been uninterrupted; but now I moved in a sphere apart, not to be profaned by the step of an outsider.

I no longer joined the boys on the playground at recess. I stayed at my desk reading some lugubrious volume— usually *The Mysteries of Udolpho*, by the amiable Mrs. Radcliffe. A translation of *The Sorrows of Werther* fell into my hands at this period, and if I could have committed suicide without killing myself, I should certainly have done so.

On half-holidays, instead of fraternizing with Pepper and the rest of our clique, I would wander off alone to Grave Point.

Grave Point—the place where Binny Wallace's body came ashore—was a narrow strip of land running out into the river. A line of Lombardy poplars, stiff and severe, like a row of grenadiers, mounted guard on the water side. On the extreme end of the peninsula was an old disused graveyard, tenanted principally by the early settlers who had been scalped by the Indians. In a remote corner of the cemetery, set apart from the other mounds, was the grave of a woman who had been hanged in the old colonial times for the murder of her infant. Goodwife Polly Haines had denied the crime to the last, and after her death there had arisen strong doubts as to her actual guilt. It was a

belief current among the lads of the town, that if you went
to this grave at nightfall on the 10th of November—the
anniversary of her execution—and asked, "For what did
the magistrates hang you?" a voice would reply,
"Nothing!"

Many a Rivermouth boy has tremblingly put this question in the dark, and, sure enough, Polly Haines invariably answered nothing!

A low red brick wall, broken down in many places and
frosted over with silvery moss, surrounded this burial
ground of our Pilgrim Fathers and their immediate de-
scendants. The latest date on any of the headstones was
1780. A crop of very funny epitaphs sprung up here and
there among the overgrown thistles and burdocks, and
almost every tablet had a death's head with cross-bones
engraved upon it, or else a puffy round face with a pair
of wings stretching out from the ears, like this:

These mortuary emblems furnished me with congenial
food for reflection. I used to lie in the long grass, and
speculate on the advantages and disadvantages of being a
cherub.

I forget what I thought the advantages were, but I remember distinctly of getting into an inextricable tangle
on two points: How could a cherub, being all head and
wings, manage to sit down when he was tired? To have to
sit down on the back of his head struck me as an awkward
alternative. Again: Where did a cherub carry those necessary articles (such as jackknives, marbles, and pieces of

twine) which boys in an earthly state of existence usually
stow away in their trousers pockets?

These were knotty questions, and I was never able to
dispose of them satisfactorily.

Meanwhile Pepper Whitcomb would scour the whole
town in search of me. He finally discovered my retreat,
one afternoon, and dropped in on me abruptly while I
was deep in the cherub problem.

"Look here, Tom Bailey!" said Pepper, shying a piece
of clamshell indignantly at the *Hic jacet* on a neighboring
gravestone, "you are just going to the dogs! Can't you
tell a fellow what in thunder ails you, instead of prowling
round among the tombs like a jolly old vampire?"

"Pepper," I replied, solemnly, "don't ask me. All is not
well here"—touching my breast mysteriously. If I had
touched my head instead, I should have been nearer the
mark.

Pepper stared at me.

"Earthly happiness," I continued, "is a delusion and
a snare. You will never be happy, Pepper, until you are
a cherub."

Pepper, by the by, would have made an excellent
cherub, he was so chubby. Having delivered myself of
these gloomy remarks, I arose languidly from the grass
and moved away, leaving Pepper staring after me in mute
astonishment. I was Hamlet and Werther and the late
Lord Byron all in one.

You will ask what my purpose was in cultivating this
factitious despondency. None whatever. Blighted Beings
never have any purpose in life excepting to be as blighted
as possible.

Of course my present line of business could not long

escape the eye of Captain Nutter. I don't know if the Captain suspected my attachment for Nelly. He never alluded to it; but he watched me. Miss Abigail watched me; Kitty Collins watched, and Sailor Ben watched me.

"I can't make out his signals," I overheard the Admiral remark to my grandfather one day. "I hope he ain't got no kind of sickness aboard."

There was something singularly agreeable in being an object of so great interest. Sometimes I had all I could do to preserve my dejected aspect, it was so pleasant to be miserable. I inclined to the opinion that people who are melancholy without any particular reason, such as poets, artists, and young musicians with long hair, have rather an enviable time of it. In a quiet way I never enjoyed myself better in my life than when I was a Blighted Being.

TWENTY

IN WHICH I PROVE MYSELF
TO BE THE GRANDSON
OF MY GRANDFATHER

IT WAS not possible for a boy of my temperament to
be a Blighted Being longer than three consecutive
weeks.

I was gradually emerging from my self-imposed cloud
when events transpired that greatly assisted in restoring
me to a more natural frame of mind. I awoke from an
imaginary trouble to face a real one.

I suppose you don't know what a financial crisis is? I
will give you an illustration. You are deeply in debt—say
to the amount of a quarter of a dollar—to the little knick-

206

knack shop round the corner, where they sell picture papers, spruce gum, needles, and Malaga raisins. A boy owes you a quarter of a dollar, which he promises to pay at a certain time. You are depending on this quarter to settle accounts with the small shopkeeper. The time arrives—and the quarter doesn't. That's a financial crisis, in one sense—in twenty-five senses, if I may say so.

When this same thing happens, on a grander scale, in the mercantile world, it produces what is called a panic. One man's inability to pay his debts ruins another man, who, in turn, ruins some one else, and so on, until failure after failure makes even the richest capitalist tremble. Public confidence is suspended, and the smaller fry of merchants are knocked over like tenpins.

These commercial panics occur periodically, after the fashion of comets and earthquakes and other disagreeable things. Such a panic took place in New Orleans in the year 18—, and my father's banking house went to pieces in the crash.

Of a comparatively large fortune, nothing remained after paying his debts excepting a few thousand dollars, with which he proposed to return North and embark in some less hazardous enterprise. In the meantime it was necessary for him to stay in New Orleans to wind up the business.

My grandfather was in some way involved in this failure, and lost, I fancy, a considerable sum of money; but he never talked much on the subject. He was an unflinching believer in the spilt-milk proverb.

"It can't be gathered up," he would say, "and it's no use crying over it. Pitch into the cow and get some more milk, is my motto."

The suspension of the banking house was bad enough, but there was an attending circumstance that gave us, at Rivermouth, a great deal more anxiety. The cholera, which some one predicted would visit the country that year, and which, indeed, had made its appearance in a mild form at several points along the Mississippi River, had broken out with much violence at New Orleans.

The report that first reached us through the newspapers was meager and contradictory; many people discredited it; but a letter from my mother left us no room for doubt. The sickness was in the city. The hospitals were filling up, and hundreds of the citizens were flying from the stricken place by every steamboat. The unsettled state of my father's affairs made it imperative for him to remain at his post; his desertion at that moment would have been at the sacrifice of all he had saved from the general wreck.

As he would be detained in New Orleans at least three months, my mother declined to come North without him.

After this we awaited with feverish impatience the weekly news that came to us from the South. The next letter advised us that my parents were well, and that the sickness, so far, had not penetrated to the faubourg, or district, where they lived. The following week brought less cheering tidings. My father's business, in consequence of the flight of the other partners, would keep him in the city beyond the period he had mentioned. The family had moved to Pass Christian, a favorite watering place on Lake Pontchartrain, near New Orleans, where he was able to spend part of each week. So the return North was postponed indefinitely.

It was now that the old longing to see my parents came

back to me with irresistible force. I knew my grandfather would not listen to the idea of my going to New Orleans at such a dangerous time, since he had opposed the journey so strongly when the same objection did not exist. But I determined to go nevertheless.

I think I have mentioned the fact that all the male members of our family, on my father's side—as far back as the Middle Ages—had exhibited in early youth a decided talent for running away. It was a hereditary talent. It ran in the blood to run away. I do not pretend to explain the peculiarity. I simply admit it.

It was not my fate to change the prescribed order of things. I, too, was to run away, thereby proving, if any proof were needed, that I was the grandson of my grandfather. I do not hold myself responsible for the step any more than I do for the shape of my nose, which is said to be a facsimile of Captain Nutter's.

When I look back now, I wonder how I had the heart to dream of stealing off from the old house and all the kindly souls it sheltered. The heart, I think, had nothing to do with it. It was a matter of destiny—and legs.

I have frequently noticed how circumstances conspire to help a man, or a boy, when he has thoroughly resolved on doing a thing. That very week the *Rivermouth Barnacle* printed an advertisement that seemed to have been written on purpose for me. It ran as follows:

WANTED.—A FEW ABLE-BODIED SEAMEN and a Cabin Boy, for the ship *Rawlings,* now loading for New Orleans at Johnson's Wharf, Boston. Apply in person, within four days, at the office of Messrs. —— —— & Co., or on board the Ship.

How I was to get to New Orleans with only $4.62 was a question that had been bothering me. This advertisement made it as clear as day. I would go as cabin boy.

I had taken Pepper into my confidence again; I had told him the story of my love for Miss Glentworth, with all its harrowing details; and now conceived it judicious to confide in him the change about to take place in my life, so that, if the *Rawlings* went down in a gale, my friends might have the limited satisfaction of knowing what had become of me.

Pepper shook his head discouragingly, and sought in every way to dissuade me from the step. He drew a disenchanting picture of the existence of a cabin boy, whose constant duty (according to Pepper) was to have dishes broken over his head whenever the captain or the mate chanced to be out of humor, which was mostly all the time. But nothing Pepper said could turn me a hair's breadth from the project.

I had little time to spare, for the advertisement stated explicitly that applications were to be made in person within four days. I trembled to think of the bare possibility of some other boy snapping up that desirable situation.

It was on Monday that I stumbled upon the advertisement. On Tuesday my preparations were completed. My baggage—consisting of four shirts, half a dozen collars, a piece of shoemaker's wax (Heaven knows what for!) and seven stockings, wrapped in a silk handkerchief—lay hidden under a loose plank of the stable floor. This was my point of departure.

My plan was to take the last train for Boston, in order to prevent the possibility of immediate pursuit, if any should be attempted. The train left at 4 P.M.

I ate no breakfast and little dinner that day. I avoided
the Captain's eye, and wouldn't have looked Miss Abigail
or Kitty in the face for the wealth of the Indies.

When it was time to start for the station I retired
quietly to the stable and uncovered my bundle. I lingered
a moment to kiss the white star on Gypsy's forehead, and
was nearly unmanned when the little animal returned the
caress by lapping my cheek. Twice I went back and patted
her.

On reaching the station I purchased my ticket with a
bravado air that ought to have aroused the suspicion of
the ticket master, and hurried to the car, where I sat
fidgeting until the train shot out into the broad daylight.

Then I drew a long breath and looked about me. The
first object that saluted my sight was Sailor Ben, four or
five seats behind me, reading the *Rivermouth Barnacle!*

Reading was not an easy art to Sailor Ben; he grappled with the sense of a paragraph as if it were a polar bear, and generally got the worst of it. On the present occasion he was having a hard struggle, judging by the way he worked his mouth and rolled his eyes. He had evidently not seen me. But what was he doing on the Boston train?

Without lingering to solve the question, I stole gently from my seat and passed into the forward car.

This was very awkward, having the Admiral on board. I couldn't understand it at all. Could it be possible that the old boy had got tired of land and was running away to sea himself? That was too absurd. I glanced nervously towards the car door now and then, half expecting to see him come after me.

We had passed one or two way-stations, and I had quieted down a good deal, when I began to feel as if somebody was looking steadily at the back of my head. I turned round involuntarily, and there was Sailor Ben again, at the further end of the car, wrestling with the *Rivermouth Barnacle* as before.

I commenced to grow very uncomfortable indeed. Was it by design or chance that he thus dogged my steps? If he was aware of my presence, why didn't he speak to me at once? Why did he steal round, making no sign, like a particularly unpleasant phantom? Maybe it *wasn't* Sailor Ben. I peeped at him slyly. There was no mistaking that tanned, genial phiz of his. Very odd he didn't see *me!*

Literature, even in the mild form of a country newspaper, always had the effect of poppies on the Admiral. When I stole another glance in his direction, his hat was tilted over his right eye in the most dissolute style, and the *Rivermouth Barnacle* lay in a confused heap beside him.

He had succumbed. He was fast, fast asleep. If he would only keep asleep until we reached our destination!

By and by I discovered that the rear car had been detached from the train at the last stopping place. This accounted satisfactorily for Sailor Ben's singular movements, and considerably calmed my fears. Nevertheless, I did not like the aspect of things.

The Admiral continued to snooze like a good fellow, and was snoring melodiously as we glided at a slackened pace over a bridge and into Boston.

I grasped my pilgrim's bundle, and, hurrying out of the car, dashed up the first street that presented itself.

It was a narrow, noisy, zigzag street, crowded with trucks and obstructed with bales and boxes of merchandise. I didn't pause to breathe until I had placed a respectable distance between me and the railway station. By this time it was nearly twilight.

I had got into the region of dwelling houses, and was about to seat myself on a doorstep to rest, when, lo! there was the Admiral trundling along on the opposite sidewalk, under a full spread of canvas, as he would have expressed it.

I was off again in an instant at a rapid pace; but in spite of all I could do he held his own without any perceptible exertion. He had a very ugly gait to get away from, the Admiral. I didn't dare to run, for fear of being mistaken for a thief, a suspicion which my bundle would naturally lend color to.

I pushed ahead, however, at a brisk trot, and must have got over one or two miles—my pursuer neither gaining nor losing ground—when I concluded to surrender at discretion. I saw that Sailor Ben was determined to have me, and, knowing my man, I knew that escape was highly improbable.

So I turned round and waited for him to catch up with me, which he did in a few seconds, looking rather sheepish at first.

"Sailor Ben," said I, severely, "do I understand that you are dogging my steps?"

"Well, little messmate," replied the Admiral, rubbing his nose, which he always did when he was disconcerted, "I *am* kind o' followin' in your wake."

"Under orders?"

"Under orders."

"Under the Captain's orders?"

"Sure-ly."

"In other words, my grandfather has sent you to fetch me back to Rivermouth?"

"That's about it," said the Admiral, with a burst of frankness.

"And I must go with you whether I want to or not?"

"The Capen's very identical words!"

There was nothing to be done. I bit my lips with suppressed anger, and signified that I was at his disposal, since I couldn't help it. The impression was very strong in my mind that the Admiral wouldn't hesitate to put me in irons if I showed signs of mutiny.

It was too late to return to Rivermouth that night—a fact which I communicated to the old boy sullenly, inquiring at the same time what he proposed to do about it.

He said we would cruise about for some rations, and
then make a night of it. I didn't condescend to reply,
though I hailed the suggestion of something to eat with
inward enthusiasm, for I had not taken enough food that
day to keep life in a canary.

We wandered back to the railway station, in the waiting
room of which was a kind of restaurant presided over by
a severe-looking young lady. Here we had a cup of coffee
apiece, several tough doughnuts, and some blocks of venerable sponge cake. The young lady who attended on us,
whatever her age was then, must have been a mere child
when that sponge cake was made.

The Admiral's acquaintance with Boston hotels was
slight; but he knew of a quiet lodging house near by, much
patronized by sea captains, and kept by a former friend
of his.

In this house, which had seen its best days, we were accommodated with a lonesome chamber containing two
cot beds, two chairs, and a cracked pitcher on a washstand. The mantel shelf was ornamented with three big
pink conch shells, resembling pieces of petrified liver; and
over these hung a cheap lurid print, in which a United
States sloop-of-war was giving a British frigate particular fits. It is very strange how our own ships never seem
to suffer any in these terrible engagements. It shows what
a nation we are.

An oil lamp on a deal table cast a dismal glare over the
apartment, which was cheerless in the extreme. I thought
of our sitting-room at home, with its flowery wallpaper
and gay curtains and soft lounges; I saw Major Elkanah
Nutter (my grandfather's father) in powdered wig and
Federal uniform, looking down benevolently from his gilt

frame between the bookcases; I pictured the Captain and Miss Abigail sitting at the cosy round table in the moon-like glow of the astral lamp; and then I fell to wondering how they would receive me when I came back. I wondered if the Prodigal Son had any idea that his father was going to kill the fatted calf for him, and how he felt about it, on the whole.

Though I was very low in spirits, I put on a bold front to Sailor Ben, you will understand. To be caught and caged in this manner was a frightful shock to my vanity. He tried to draw me into conversation; but I answered in icy monosyllables. He again suggested we should make a night of it, and hinted broadly that he was game for any amount of riotous dissipation, even to the extent of going to see a play if I wanted to. I declined haughtily. I was dying to go.

He then threw out a feeler on the subject of dominos and checkers, and observed in a general way that "seven-up" was a capital game; but I repulsed him at every point.

I saw that the Admiral was beginning to feel hurt at my systematic coldness. We had always been such hearty friends until now. It was too bad of me to fret that tender, honest old heart even for an hour. I really did love the ancient boy, and when, in a disconsolate way, he ordered up a pitcher of beer, I unbent so far as to partake of some in a teacup. He recovered his spirits instantly, and took out his cuddy clay pipe for a smoke.

Between the beer and the soothing fragrance of the navy plug, I fell into a pleasanter mood myself, and, it being too late now to go to the theater, I condescended to say—addressing the northwest corner of the ceiling—that "seven-up" *was* a capital game. Upon this hint the Admiral disappeared, and returned shortly with a very dirty pack of cards.

As we played, with varying fortunes, by the flickering flame of the lamp, he sipped his beer and became communicative. He seemed immensely tickled by the fact that I had come to Boston. It leaked out presently that he and the Captain had had a wager on the subject.

The discovery of my plans and who had discovered them were points on which the Admiral refused to throw any light. They had been discovered, however, and the Captain had laughed at the idea of my running away. Sailor Ben, on the contrary, had stoutly contended that I meant to slip cable and be off. Whereupon the Captain offered to bet him a dollar that I wouldn't go. And it was partly on account of this wager that Sailor Ben refrained from capturing me when he might have done so at the start.

Now, as the fare to and from Boston, with lodging expenses, would cost him at least five dollars, I didn't see what he gained by winning the wager. The Admiral rubbed his nose violently when this view of the case presented itself.

I asked him why he didn't take me from the train at the first stopping place and return to Rivermouth by the down train at 4:30. He explained: having purchased a ticket for Boston, he considered himself bound to the owners (the stockholders of the road) to fulfill his part of the contract!

This struck me as being so deliciously funny, that after I was in bed and the light was out, I couldn't help laughing aloud once or twice. I suppose the Admiral must have thought I was meditating another escape, for he made periodical visits to my bed throughout the night, satisfying himself by kneading me all over that I hadn't evaporated.

I was all there, however, the next morning, when Sailor Ben half awakened me by shouting merrily, "All hands on deck!" The words rang in my ears like a part of my own dream, for I was at that instant climbing up the side of the *Rawlings* to offer myself as cabin boy for the voyage.

The Admiral was obliged to shake me two or three times before he could detach me from the dream. I opened my eyes with effort, and stared stupidly round the room. Bit by bit my real situation dawned on me. What a sickening sensation that is, when one is in trouble, to wake up feeling free for a moment, and then to find yesterday's sorrow all ready to go on again!

"Well, little messmate, how fares it?"

I was too much depressed to reply. The thought of returning to Rivermouth chilled me. How could I face Captain Nutter, to say nothing of Miss Abigail and Kitty? How the Temple Grammar School boys would look at me! How Conway and Seth Rodgers would exult over my mortification! And what if the Rev. Wibird Hawkins should allude to me publicly, as "an awful example of total depravity," in his next Sunday's sermon? Sailor Ben was wise in keeping an eye on me, for after these thoughts took possession of my mind, I wanted only the opportunity to give him the slip.

The keeper of the lodgings did not supply meals to his guests; so we breakfasted at a small chophouse in a crooked street on our way to the cars. The city was not astir yet, and looked glum and careworn in the damp morning atmosphere.

Here and there as we passed along was a sharp-faced shop boy taking down shutters; and now and then we met a seedy man who had evidently spent the night in a door-way. Such early birds and a few laborers with their tin kettles were the only signs of life to be seen until we came to the station, where I insisted on paying for my own ticket. I didn't relish being conveyed from place to place, like a felon changing prisons, at somebody else's expense.

On entering the car I sunk into a seat next the window, and Sailor Ben deposited himself beside me, cutting off all chance of escape.

The car filled up soon after this, and I wondered if there was anything in my mien that would lead the other passengers to suspect I was a boy who had run away and was being brought back.

A man in front of us—he was nearsighted, as I discovered later by his reading a guidebook with his nose—brought the blood to my cheeks by turning round and peering at me steadily. I rubbed a clear spot on the cloudy windowglass at my elbow, and looked out to avoid him.

There, in the travelers' room, was the severe-looking young lady piling up her blocks of sponge cake in allur-ing pyramids and industriously intrenching herself be-hind a breastwork of squash pie. I saw with cynical pleasure numerous victims walk up to the counter and recklessly sow the seeds of death in their constitutions by eating her doughnuts. I had got quite interested in her, when the whistle sounded and the train began to move.

The Admiral and I did not talk much on the journey.

I stared out of the window most of the time, speculating at to the probable nature of the reception in store for me at the terminus of the road.

What would the Captain say? and Mr. Grimshaw, what would he do about it? Then I thought of Pepper Whitcomb. Dire was the vengeance I meant to wreak on Pepper, for who but he had betrayed me? Pepper alone had been the repository of my secret—perfidious Pepper!

As we left station after station behind us, I felt less and less like encountering the members of our family. Sailor Ben fathomed what was passing in my mind, for he leaned over and said,

"I don't think as the Capen will bear down very hard on you."

But it wasn't that. It wasn't the fear of any physical punishment that might be inflicted; it was a sense of my own folly that was creeping over me; for during the long, silent ride I had examined my conduct from every standpoint, and there was no view I could take of myself in which I did not look like a very foolish person indeed.

As we came within sight of the spires of Rivermouth, I wouldn't have cared if the up train, which met us outside the town, had run into us and ended me.

Contrary to my expectation and dread, the Captain was not visible when we stepped from the cars. Sailor Ben glanced among the crowd of faces, apparently looking for him too. Conway was there—he was always hanging about the station—and if he had intimated in any way that he knew of my disgrace and enjoyed it, I should have walked into him, I am certain.

But this defiant feeling entirely deserted me by the

time we reached the Nutter House. The Captain himself opened the door.

"Come on board, sir," said Sailor Ben, scraping his left foot and touching his hat sea-fashion.

My grandfather nodded to Sailor Ben, somewhat coldly I thought, and much to my astonishment kindly took me by the hand.

I was unprepared for this, and the tears, which no amount of severity would have wrung from me, welled up to my eyes.

The expression of my grandfather's face, as I glanced at it hastily, was grave and gentle; there was nothing in it of anger or reproof. I followed him into the sitting-room, and, obeying a motion of his hand, seated myself on the sofa. He remained standing by the round table for a moment, lost in thought, then leaned over and picked up a letter.

It was a letter with a great black seal.

IN WHICH I LEAVE RIVERMOUTH

A LETTER with a great black seal!
I knew then what had happened as well as I
know it now. But which was it, father or mother? I do not
like to look back to the agony and suspense of that moment.

My father had died at New Orleans during one of his
weekly visits to the city. The letter bearing these tidings
had reached Rivermouth the evening of my flight—had
passed me on the road by the down train.

I must turn back for a moment to that eventful evening. When I failed to make my appearance at supper,
the Captain began to suspect that I had really started on
my wild tour southward—a conjecture which Sailor Ben's
absence helped to confirm. I had evidently got off by the
train and Sailor Ben had followed me.

There was no telegraphic communication between Boston and Rivermouth in those days; so my grandfather
could do nothing but await the result. Even if there had

been another mail to Boston, he could not have availed himself of it, not knowing how to address a message to the fugitives. The post office was naturally the last place either I or the Admiral would think of visiting.

My grandfather, however, was too full of trouble to allow this to add to his distress. He knew that the faithful old sailor would not let me come to any harm, and, even if I had managed for the time being to elude him, was sure to bring me back sooner or later.

Our return, therefore, by the first train on the following day did not surprise him.

I was greatly puzzled, as I have said, by the gentle manner of his reception; but when we were alone together in the sitting-room, and he began slowly to unfold the letter, I understood it all. I caught a sight of my mother's handwriting in the superscription, and there was nothing left to tell me.

My grandfather held the letter a few seconds irresolutely, and then commenced reading it aloud; but he could get no further than the date.

"I can't read it, Tom," said the old gentleman, breaking down. "I thought I could."

He handed it to me. I took the letter mechanically, and hurried away with it to my little room, where I had passed so many happy hours.

The week that followed the receipt of this letter is nearly a blank in my memory. I remember that the days appeared endless; that at times I could not realize the misfortune that had befallen us, and my heart upbraided me for not feeling a deeper grief; that a full sense of my loss would now and then sweep over me like an inspiration, and I would steal away to my chamber or wander forlornly about the gardens. I remember this, but little more.

As the days went by my first grief subsided, and in its place grew up a want which I have experienced at every step in life from boyhood to manhood. Often, even now, after all these years, when I see a lad of twelve or fourteen walking by his father's side, and glancing merrily up at his face, I turn and look after them, and am conscious that I have missed companionship most sweet and sacred.

I shall not dwell on this portion of my story, which, like the old year, is drawing to an end. There were many tranquil, pleasant hours in store for me at that period, and I prefer to turn to them.

One evening the Captain came smiling into the sitting-room with an open letter in his hand. My mother had arrived at New York, and would be with us the next day. For the first time in weeks—years, it seemed to me— something of the old cheerfulness mingled with our conversation round the evening lamp. I was to go to Boston with the Captain to meet her and bring her home. I need not describe that meeting. With my mother's hand in mine once more, all the long years we had been parted appeared like a dream. Very dear to me was the sight of that slender, pale woman passing from room to room, and lending a patient grace and beauty to the saddened life of the old house.

Everything was changed with us now. There were consultations with lawyers, and signing of papers, and correspondence; for my father's affairs had been left in great confusion. And when these were settled, the evenings were

not long enough for us to hear all my mother had to tell of
the scenes she had passed through in the ill-fated city.

Then there were old times to talk over, full of remi-
niscences of Aunt Chloe and little Black Sam. Little Black
Sam, by the by, had been taken by his master from my
father's service ten months previously, and put on a sugar
plantation near Baton Rouge. Not relishing the change,
Sam had run away, and by some mysterious agency got
into Canada, from which place he had sent back several
indecorous messages to his late owner. Aunt Chloe was still
in New Orleans, employed as nurse in one of the cholera
hospital wards, and the Desmoulins, near neighbors of
ours, had purchased the pretty stone house among the
orange trees.

How all these simple details interested me will be readily
understood by any boy who has been long absent from
home.

I was sorry when it became necessary to discuss questions more nearly affecting myself. I had been removed
from school temporarily, but it was decided, after much
consideration, that I should not return, the decision being
left, in a manner, in my own hands.

The Captain wished to carry out his son's intention and
send me to college, for which I was nearly fitted; but our
means did not admit of this. The Captain, too, could ill
afford to bear the expense, for his losses by the failure of
the New Orleans business had been heavy. Yet he insisted
on the plan, not seeing clearly what other disposal to make
of me.

In the midst of our discussions a letter came from my
Uncle Snow, a merchant in New York, generously offer-

ing me a place in his counting house. The case resolved
itself into this: if I went to college, I should have to be
dependent on Captain Nutter for several years, and at
the end of the collegiate course would have no settled profession. If I accepted my uncle's offer, I might hope to
work my way to independence without loss of time. It was
hard to give up the long-cherished dream of being a Har-
vard boy; but I gave it up.

The decision once made, it was Uncle Snow's wish that
I should enter his counting house immediately. The cause
of my good uncle's haste was this—he was afraid that I
would turn out to be a poet before he could make a merchant of me. His fears were based upon the fact that I had
published in the *Rivermouth Barnacle* some verses addressed in a familiar manner "To the Moon." Now, the
idea of a boy, with his living to get, placing himself in
communication with the Moon, struck the mercantile mind
as monstrous. It was not only a bad investment, it was
lunacy.

We adopted Uncle Snow's views so far as to accede to
his proposition forthwith. My mother, I neglected to say,
was also to reside in New York.

I shall not draw a picture of Pepper Whitcomb's disgust when the news was imparted to him, nor attempt to
paint Sailor Ben's distress at the prospect of losing his
little messmate.

In the excitement of preparing for the journey I didn't
feel any very deep regret myself. But when the moment
came for leaving, and I saw my small trunk lashed up behind the carriage, then the pleasantness of the old life and
a vague dread of the new came over me, and a mist filled
my eyes, shutting out the group of schoolfellows, includ-

ing all the members of the Centipede Club, who had come
down to the house to see me off.

As the carriage swept round the corner, I leaned out of
the window to take a last look at Sailor Ben's cottage, and
there was the Admiral's flag flying at half-mast!

So I left Rivermouth, little dreaming that I was not to
see the old place again for many and many a year.

TWENTY-TWO

EXEUNT OMNES

WITH the close of my school days at Rivermouth this modest chronicle ends.

The new life upon which I entered, the new friends and foes I encountered on the road, and what I did and what I did not, are matters that do not come within the scope of these pages. But before I write Finis to the record as it stands, before I leave it—feeling as if I were once more going away from my boyhood—I have a word or two to say concerning a few of the personages who have figured in the story, if you will allow me to call Gypsy a personage.

I am sure that the reader who has followed me thus far will be willing to hear what became of her, and Sailor Ben and Miss Abigail and the Captain.

First about Gypsy. A month after my departure from Rivermouth the Captain informed me by letter that he had parted with the little mare, according to agreement. She had been sold to the ring master of a traveling circus (I had stipulated on this disposal of her), and was about to set out on her travels. She did not disappoint my glow-

ing anticipations, but became quite a celebrity in her way
—by dancing the polka to slow music on a pine-board ball-
room constructed for the purpose.

I chanced once, a long while afterwards, to be in a
country town where her troup was giving exhibitions; I
even read the gaudily illumined show bill, setting forth the
accomplishments of

The far-famed Arabian Trick Pony,

ZULEIKA!!

FORMERLY OWNED BY

THE PRINCE SHAZ-ZAMAN OF DAMASCUS

—but failed to recognize my dear little Mustang girl behind those high-sounding titles, and so, alas! did not
attend the performance.

I hope all the praises she received and all the spangled
trappings she wore did not spoil her; but I am afraid they
did, for she was always over much given to the vanities of
this world!

Miss Abigail regulated the domestic destinies of my
grandfather's household until the day of her death, which
Dr. Theophilus Tredick solemnly averred was hastened
by the inveterate habit she had contracted of swallowing
unknown quantities of hot drops whenever she fancied herself out of sorts. Eighty-seven empty phials were found in
a bonnet box on a shelf in her bedroom closet.

The old house became very lonely when the family got
reduced to Captain Nutter and Kitty; and when Kitty
passed away, my grandfather divided his time between
Rivermouth and New York.

Sailor Ben did not long survive his little Irish lass, as he always fondly called her. At his demise, which took place about six years since, he left his property in trust to the managers of a "Home for Aged Mariners." In his will, which was a very whimsical document—written by himself, and worded with much shrewdness, too—he warned the Trustees that when he got "aloft" he intended to keep his "weather eye" on them, and should send "a speritual shot across their bows" and bring them to, if they didn't treat the Aged Mariners handsomely.

He also expressed a wish to have his body stitched up in a shotted hammock and dropped into the harbor; but as he did not strenuously insist on this, and as it was not in accordance with my grandfather's preconceived notions of Christian burial, the Admiral was laid to rest beside Kitty, in the Old South Burying Ground, with an anchor that would have delighted him neatly carved on his headstone.

I am sorry the fire has gone out in the old ship's stove in that sky-blue cottage at the head of the wharf; I am sorry they have taken down the flagstaff and painted over the funny portholes; for I loved the old cabin as it was. They might have let it alone!

For several months after leaving Rivermouth I carried on a voluminous correspondence with Pepper Whitcomb; but it gradually dwindled down to a single letter a month, and then to none at all. But while he remained at the Temple Grammar School he kept me advised of the current gossip of the town and the doings of the Centipedes.

As one by one the boys left the academy—Adams, Harris, Marden, Blake, and Langdon—to seek their fortunes elsewhere, there was less to interest me in the old seaport; and when Pepper himself went to Philadelphia to read law, I had no one to give me an inkling of what was going on.

There wasn't much to go on, to be sure. Great events no longer considered it worth their while to honor so quiet a place. One Fourth of July the Temple Grammar School burnt down—set fire, it was supposed, by an eccentric squib that was seen to bolt into an upper window—and Mr. Grimshaw retired from public life, married, "and lived happily ever after," as the storybooks say.

The widow Conway, I am able to state, did not succeed in enslaving Mr. Meeks, the apothecary, who united himself clandestinely to one of Miss Dorothy Gibbs's young ladies, and lost the patronage of Primrose Hall in consequence.

Young Conway went into the grocery business with his ancient chum, Rodgers—RODGERS & CONWAY! I read the sign only last summer when I was down in Rivermouth, and had half a mind to pop into the shop and shake hands with him, and ask him if he wanted to fight. I contented myself, however, with flattening my nose against his dingy shop window, and beheld Conway, in red whiskers and blue overalls, weighing out sugar for a customer—giving him short weight, I'll bet anything!

I have reserved my pleasantest word for the last. It is touching the Captain. The Captain is still hale and rosy, and if he doesn't relate his exploit in the War of 1812 as spiritedly as he used to, he makes up by relating it more frequently and telling it differently every time! He passes his winters in New York and his summers in the Nutter House, which threatens to prove a hard nut for the destructive gentleman with the scythe and the hourglass, for the seaward gable has not yielded a clapboard to the

east wind these twenty years. The Captain has now become
the Oldest Inhabitant in Rivermouth, and so I don't laugh
at the Oldest Inhabitant any more, but pray in my heart
that he may occupy the post of honor for half a century
to come!

So ends the Story of a Bad Boy—but not such a very
bad boy, as I told you to begin with.

FINIS

DATE DUE	

GAYLORD   PRINTED IN U.S.A.